ALSO BY KAT & STONE BASTION

THE TRAVELER: Initiate Years

Veil of Realms · Secrets of Alexandria · Panther Rising
Stones of Power · Highland Magick

Highland Legends Series

Forged in Dreams and Magick · Bound by Wish and Mistletoe
Born of Mist and Legend · Found in Flame and Moonlight

Unbreakable Series

Heartbreaker · Rule Breaker · Lawbreaker
Forthcoming: *Ball Breaker · Icebreaker*

No Weddings Series

No Weddings · One Funeral
Two Bar Mitzvahs · Three Christmases
For Valentine's

Standalone Novels & Novelettes

Brand New Year · The Espionage Effect

Romantic Poetry for Charity

Utterly Loved

Forged in Dreams and Magick

First Place – Unpublished Beacon Award
Best Paranormal Romance

First Place – Hold Me, Thrill Me Award
Best Paranormal Romance

Chosen by FreshFiction.com as their Fresh Pick for October 22, 2013

"A beautifully woven tale about love, choices, courage and destiny, *Forged in Dreams and Magick* is one of the best time-traveling novels. Fans of Gabaldon's *Outlander* will love it."

- BOOKISH TEMPTATIONS

"I was gripping my iPad like a crazy woman and fanning myself from the smoldering romance. Lawdy!"

- THE FLIRTY READER

"Bastion's debut is pure perfection, a combination of romance, magic, emotion, adventure and surprising twists and turns. This is a truly unique romance that should not be missed!"

"HOLY HELL!!! I am so... um... wow! FABULOUSNESS. *Forged in Dreams and Magick* definitely makes my BEST OF list for 2013..."

"A story guaranteed to enthrall with lushly detailed travels into times long gone by. Woven with love, passion, magic and legend, the story had me hooked from the very first chapter."

"Kat Bastion's wonderful debut brings a new voice to the fore. Her voice is strong and unhesitating, very human and real, sometimes young and delicious in her treatment of intimacy and relationship development."

"OMG, Bastion hits all cylinders in this supernatural tale. The layers in the book were fascinating, and I devoured the fun, adventuresome read."

Bound by Wish and Mistletoe

"I LOVED it! *Bound by Wish and Mistletoe* is, to my mind, a perfect entry in the historical / paranormal fiction genre and has quite a bit to offer."

"Kat Bastion has done it again! ... Excellent holiday novella, perfect for a cup of cocoa and snuggling under a blanket in front of the fireplace this holiday season."

"Move over, Julia Quinn and Sabrina Jeffries! Kat Bastion is an absolutely gifted author and deserves to be recognized for her talent."

Heartbreaker

"This book has definitely earned its five stars and I am just floored right now. The passion is explosive, the story itself is beautiful, and the emotions are so real my heart is ready to burst. Beautiful book. Absolutely breathtaking."

- ONE PAGE AT A TIME

"Heartrending, passionate, and captivating! *Heartbreaker* is a riveting page-turner that will leave you breathless with raw emotions, and the need to hold tight to the ones you love!"

- BENEATH THE COVERS BLOG

"This book is all about flawless writing, exemplary storytelling, f*#king insane character development. The right dose of sexy hotness..."

- LOVE N. BOOKS

"The Bastions are at it again with this beautiful and heartbreaking story. You will absolutely fall in love with Kiki and Darren's love."

- UNDER THE COVERS BOOK BLOG

"*Heartbreaker* is a phenomenal story."

"I loved it...wonderfully compelling, a story that touched my heart in so many ways and characters I will remember for a long time to come."

No Weddings and
THE NO WEDDINGS SERIES

"One of the best romantic comedies of the year!"

"The No Weddings series is one of the best I have read that follows one couple. Cade and Hannah are both lovable characters, the storyline is real and entertaining, and the banter is fun and witty."

"I loved it, and I mean REALLY loved it!"

"This is an exceptional series... You find yourself fully engrossed in their world and can't put the book down."

"The No Weddings series has a group of such amazing characters; you can't help but relate to them and feel the emotion in every situation they encounter. It has been a long time since a story has made me feel that way let alone an entire series!"

"The story of Cade & Hannah's relationship is realistic, heart-warming, and filled with real-world connections that shook me in a way that few titles I've read this year have managed...I have loved every minute of the No Weddings series."

BRAVING SOTERIA

BRAVING SOTERIA

A QUANTANAUTS COLLECTION

KAT BASTION

INTRODUCTION

What inspires a romance writer like me to veer into science fiction with five original stories?

Well, technically, my award-winning debut novel, *Forged in Dreams and Magick*, catapults a feisty Southern California heroine through time. So I actually began writing romance through a science fiction (fantasy) framework.

But, oh...

I possess a *fierce* love for science fiction and deep space, and have all my life.

Beginning with the original Star Trek series as a kid.

Tribbles!

But then George Lucas gifted us with his original Star Wars trilogy. Which I watched with wide-eyed wonder as an eight-year-old in 1977. At the historic Cine Capri in Phoenix, Arizona.

Trivia Factoid: The Cine Capri played *Star Wars* for over a year, which ended up being the movie's longest run in North America.

And as an early science geek, due to both of those influences, and many others, space discoveries have always fascinated me. Destructive black holes. Mesmerizing watercolor nebulas. Earth-threatening asteroids.

I'm still drawn to articles about deep space. Especially the periodic reassessing of all the things scientists don't know. While our insatiable hunger for knowledge grows, inspiring us to push our boundaries and explore new worlds.

Later came the heart-pounding (and heartwarming) blockbuster *Armageddon*. With its ragtag team of oil drillers, drafted as Earth's last hope against a giant asteroid threatening Earth.

Modern Star Trek movies further whet my appetite for space exploration, with fantastic actors and brilliant adventures as their courageous crew defied all odds to accomplish their missions.

But...

What happens when Earth faces *total destruction* from an asteroid before our greatest minds formulate a viable defense plan?

What if no escape route exists... *out there?*

It's not farfetched to imagine our space programs simply run out of time.

The dinosaurs got wiped out.

What makes us think we're exempt?

In fact, one of Earth's weapons in planetary defense, got completely destroyed in December 2020 when the telescope's deteriorating instrument platform plummeted into the dish below, support towers, cables and all.

That massive radio telescope, Puerto Rico's Arecibo Observatory, had been making space discoveries for almost sixty years. It had been made famous in the James Bond film *Goldeneye* and Jodie Foster's *Contact*.

Arecibo had also determined the three-hundred-meter

asteroid Apophis will get so close to Earth, it's expected to fly between our outer communications satellites and the planet in 2029.

Talk about bullet burn!

Sooo... yeah.

With that wonderful foundation of science fiction fascination, my imagination exploded.

What if Earth can't escape a planet-killer asteroid?

What would humankind do?

Who will step up to save our species from annihilation?

Read on to find out.

Five original stories, written specifically for this collection.

With great pleasure, I introduce you to our brave... *Quantanauts*.

I hope you enjoy their stories.

Kat Bastion

CAUSTIC

The gaping maw of space and time yawned three meters directly above the trio of brave explorers. Pitch black and daunting. Cavernous and endless.

Threatening.

Inspiring.

And the most significant phenomenon on planet Earth.

A last-ditch hope of saving humankind... from mass extinction.

Celeste Kaminski swallowed hard, attempting soothe a throat gone bone dry. Instinctual terror gripped her, pulse quickening, breaths shallowing. Black dots began to fringe her vision.

Till her clingy custom-made environmental suit blasted vital-signs warnings into its helmet. Red lights flashed on the upper-right of her visor. Alarm bells clanged in her ears.

Calm. She pinched her eyes shut, banishing the fear as she drew in a slow lungful of air. Causing the warning system to cycle back off. *You've been trained for this.*

NASA and the new military branch Alt-Realm—with over a thousand leading scientists gathered from around the globe—monitored her team from an oblong perimeter, perched at stations in a stadium array of cutting-edge technology. All housed inside the world's largest military hangar, a brand-new dome constructed of steel and concrete and, apparently, top-secret materials. Everyone vetted for the highest levels of clearance. And sworn to the utmost secrecy.

The warm humid air in her helmet developed a sour tang as she began to sweat.

When she licked her lips, a taste of salt laced the tip of her tongue.

Low rasping, her own breathing, filled the stretching void of established radio silence.

And for one beautiful moment, the greatest thing in her world flashed into her mind: Liam. Her five-year-old son, the beautiful curly-dark-haired inquisitive boy who'd been taken to kindergarten that morning by a helpful neighbor. The reason she risked her life, even as a single parent.

Because for Liam to have a future, the mission had to succeed.

To rescue all their children.

Yet even with the greatest minds in the world tapped for the event, no one knew the odds of their success. Or survival.

And once the phenomenon above them had activated seconds ago—for her team's first real mission—she'd been unable to fully settle her nerves. Maybe for the better. Kept her sharp.

Green-lit data flashed onto her visor. The atmosphere above had cooled. Considerably.

And what she saw... blew her mind.

No one had yet identified what anyone viewed through the phenomenon's membrane Earth-side.

Celeste watched the solid inky expanse shift into a fluid blackness, more saturated in the center, fading to midnight blackish-blue toward the edges. Glimmers of light sparkled in myriad swirling colors, thick and rich. But not as stars twinkle in a nighttime sky. More like iridescent rainbows reflected from oil on water... that shimmered with multilayered depth.

Of course, there'd been multiple theories tossed about regarding the exact nature of the invented discovery. The stretch of a billion galaxies stacked atop one another? Countless alternates of Earth's present reality? Interdimensional gateway to parallel realms?

Not that the exact definition of the oddity made one bit of difference.

Because, for better or worse, the human race had passed a point of no return.

And in response, NASA and Alt-Realm had unleashed what the fearmongering media had begun to coin Pandora's Box.

An unimaginable danger? Without doubt.

But humankind had run out of options. And in a last act of desperation, had intentionally conjured the mysterious gateway.

In the hopes of evacuating what they could of the planet.

Because all life on Earth was doomed.

Thanks to the planet-killer asteroid hurtling toward them: Thanatos, Deliverer of Death.

Which had somehow escaped everyone's notice. Until the deflection window—the time needed to exercise Earth's defense options to affect the asteroid or its trajectory—had slipped right by.

Time remaining before impact? Six weeks.

Down to the wire.

But NASA, Alt-Realm, and those global scientists had needed every single second of the last nine months. Not only to build the massive hangar. But to create their actual world-bending phenomenon. From one lone car-sized prototype. Into its mindboggling full size, three hundred meters long and half as wide.

The minimum size required, according to experts, to relocate enough of their species. And give those colonists heading into worlds unknown some kind of fighting chance.

Named Soteria—after the goddess of salvation and deliverance—the mechanism curved like a snaking tunnel into an infinity-like shape. Its outer membrane, an opaque dark-gray, shifted translucent when activated to reveal that cold gaping maw of time and space.

Soteria had been created by somehow combining the brainpower of quantum pioneers, a unique mix of rare earth minerals, and the enlightened vision of one brilliant soul who had devised a way to pierce through our dimension.

All while five three-person teams had been assembled and trained for the quantum jump. They were called quantanauts.

Celeste's team had been chosen as the first colonist scout team to make the jump.

To her left towered Commander Braden Moore, team strategist, meteorologist, and military muscle. On her right bounced the leanly built Corporal Cara Lightner, general surgeon, sharpshooter, and savant linguist.

Celeste had been drafted as the sole non-military member of their crew: zoologist, botanist, and hobby theorist in all things extraterrestrial.

All three had different skin colors and looks by design: to represent a mix of the migrating populace to any intelligent alien life. Bald all-American Braden had a rich dark complexion. Cara, with a Scandinavian father and Japanese mother, had raven hair shorn into short curls and porcelain white skin. Celeste, with her melting-pot heritage of Israeli, Italian, Native American, and Russian, skewed toward a medium tanned olive with a head of wavy brunette hair.

Not that any of that could be seen while fully suited with helmets on.

But in the hopes that first contact with intelligent life might be made. And peaceful relations could be established.

Maybe that the natives might even lend a helping hand.

Instead of their viewing the initial presence of armed scouts, followed by a mass exodus of millions (all Alt-Realm figured they had time for), as an invasion.

In preparation for their mission, over the last five months, all quantanauts had received a crash-course training in everything under the sun. From survival skills and combat warfare to mechanical repair and data analysis. Inside the harshest environments imaginable. With every conceivable worst-case scenario examined, plotted, and planned.

With each member, emphasis had been placed on general medical skills and military cross training. Because, if two team members got wounded (or killed) in a firefight, the third had to be able to defend them, patch up the wounded (or drag the dead), and bring everyone home.

Home.

The whole concept of that word had shifted for her.

Since home existed somewhere... out there.

With a sudden hard whomp of vibration, the moment they'd all been waiting for arrived.

The black rainbow shimmering pulsed, causing those myriad pinpricks of color to swirl into various eddies.

An instant later, their pre-mission probe dropped out ten meters ahead of them. Decelerating as it plummeted, it stopped and hovered just above the concrete floor.

The size of a basketball, its titanium surface appeared iced over.

And a reddish orange slime glistened on one side.

"Well," Braden said. "That's new."

Contamination from another world. The three of them all wore environmental suits. However, the scientists had chosen as a group not to shield themselves. No matter how hard Celeste had tried to argue the danger. Saw the possibility of the project ending before it began.

The retort from Admiral Worthington and his official decision on the matter: *If this doesn't work, we're all dead anyway.*

She'd stifled a smartass comeback about costs, foresight, and lack of contingency planning. Because that's what it amounted to. None of those brilliant minds designing their hangar had given consideration to what they'd be bringing through. Everyone had been focusing on the mass exodus's one-way transport out.

"Still a go?" Cara asked, staring at the slimed probe.

Each of the three had received the same telemetry from the drone through their visors as soon it popped back into their world. Environmental readings on everything from temperature and wind speed to gravity fluctuations and radiation levels.

"Kaminski?" he asked.

Celeste double-checked every reading the probe had gathered of the world it had been in. The awaiting environment remained the same as their prior two days of three probes apiece, one each morning, midday, and evening leading up to their mission. They'd checked light levels at certain Earth times (no correlation observed.) And verified atmospheric oxygen mix (a touch high on the oxygen side, but livable.)

"World is the same," Celeste replied. "But no telemetry on the ice or slime on the probe itself. It's as if the substances don't exist."

"What the hell does that mean?" Cara squatted down beside the probe, examining the slime closer.

"Don't touch it!" Celeste warned. They had no idea what that stuff was. Sometimes the tiniest biological things wielded the mightiest defense mechanisms.

Cara popped back upright, raising her hands in surrender. "Not about to."

Braden tilted his head.

All Celeste could see of his face, due to the bright spotlights in the stadium shining down on them, was a slight silhouette... no facial expression.

"Did the substance interfere with our technology?" he asked.

"Possibly." Celeste shrugged. "But without time to analyze, we have no way of knowing."

"Rest of the readings look good," Cara said. "I'm a *go*.'"

Celeste took a deep breath thinking of Liam. They were taking insane risks with their lives. In order to save millions more.

Fortified by her purpose, she gave their commander a nod. "I'm a *go*."

Then she glanced right, at a larger structure about three stories up that cantilevered apart from the rest of the stadium of scientists, perching closer to the action below. Where the command center resided.

"Control, we have a *go*," Braden advised.

"Confirm *go* status," Admiral Worthington said.

7

"Programming that slimed drone to come back with us," Braden said.

They already had three others hovering behind where they stood, programmed to take the leap with them. Along with three cases of gear with weaponry strapped to it, under the protection of a large inflatable for a safe landing. Every last item having identity nanotech homing chips linked to Soteria, similar to the ones woven into their environmental suits.

"And time count?" Braden called.

"Three..." Cara started.

"Two..." Celeste followed.

"One," the commander said.

On the next beat, they crouched down as one, then jumped high, arms fully extended above them.

At the last moment, as her muscles bunched then punched her up with power, Celeste cast out a wish to Liam. For his safety and well-being, come what may.

And for her team's own safety and success.

Then with a strange sizzling sensation, her fingertips breached the invisible membrane of Soteria.

And the dark gaping maw of space and time sucked them into some unknown world.

―――――――――

An enormous vastness bled into Celeste's consciousness.

While white-hot fire ignited every nerve ending.

The pain so great at first, she couldn't breathe.

An instant later, her awareness heightened... but she'd lost all connection with her body. Wouldn't have a clue whether she physically breathed or not.

The fluid blackness remained. With its swirling oil-slick pinpricks of light. And blackish midnight horizon.

Only she didn't actually "see" it any longer.

Somehow, she'd become a part of its iridescence.

Countless hues of light and vibrations permeated her mind, yet nothing formed a whole. No recognition. Nothing computed into her understanding with any kind of form or substance.

All her memories remained intact, though. And she thought to communicate to her team.

But she had no vocal cords.

And yet, with concentration, she sensed Braden and Cara there. Through the blackness. Although she had no idea how. Maybe through a combined consciousness.

Peace washed over her as she gave herself over to the process.

Thoughts bounced around, buoyant and free.

Out of control of her physical body, her mind remained all she had for whatever time their travel took.

Time. Such a crazy thing.

Earth's time wound down on a doomsday clock.

What would Liam think of the oil-slick multicolored blackness? Of Soteria, their goddess gateway to other worlds? Of thinking and being, but without a body.

How many others could the mysterious portal transport at once?

The sensation of her teammates seemed good, light.

Would thousands of evacuees at a time—all together at once—feel the same?

Blackness and rainbow pinpricks swirled in her mind, around her, through her.

She remembered what the scientists had shared during their crash-course quantanaut training. The short history of

Soteria. That they knew nothing about where they were jumping to. Not where. Not when.

In early experiments, scientists had simply tossed a probe in.

Which they never saw again.

Those brilliant minds kept at it, with slightly modified probes. From different entry trajectories. Again and again. Disappointed with each failed attempt. But hopeful and determined, because they had no backup option. They tried, tested, recorded, and tweaked. Before trying again. For months.

Eventually, they'd learned to tag the probe with a nanotech homing chip made of the same rare earth minerals as Soteria. And even though communications were impossible through the gateway, they'd been successful in sending a pulse of energy through the gateway to call the probe back.

Most of the time.

Why they'd sent half a dozen verification probes, plus the pre-jump orange-slimed probe, before Team One's trip.

But in the months before that morning, they'd send tens of thousands of probes in. Sometimes hours apart. As fast as countries around the world could build the probes, they'd toss them up into Soteria. All tagged with those nanotech homing chips.

The scientists theorized that each probe which popped back to Earth did so because it had arrived safely in an environment that hadn't destroyed it.

And in those tens of thousands of attempts, only eighty-seven probes had returned.

Of the eighty-seven, five alone had goldilocks worlds. Those just-right conditions needed to sustain human life. An atmosphere. Decent temperature. The right mix of oxygen. Similar gravity. Water molecules. Soil samples. Evidence of plant life, even if through seeds or spores.

Five goldilocks worlds?

Required five teams of quantanauts.

Quantanauts in the loosest sense of the word. They all hoped.

Named so only because quantum theories had been the genesis foundation for creating Soteria.

No one relished the idea of breaking apart into their billions of infinitesimal particles in transport, then reassembling into a whole person again on some other side.

Because... what if someone got stitched back together wrong?

But something else entirely happened with Soteria, or so they all thought. A shortcut into galaxies? Definitely some kind of wormhole tunnel, transporting the probes (and hopefully millions of evacuees) from one place to the next.

Later, after the colonists established a new home, those scientists could spend the rest of their lives testing out their theories.

Till then, they jumped blindly into the dark, with educated guesses and hopes for the best.

She thought about her quantanaut team again. Sensed them there. Somewhere. Calm, like her. Reflective, perhaps.

Then she wondered what kind of readings her environmental suit received.

Without eyes to see or ears to hear, no sense of smell, touch, or taste, the warning flashing lights and clanging bells could be going off, and she wouldn't detect a thing.

However, with the soothing sensation of surrounding peace, of being one with the fluid darkness, she thought not.

Instead, she embraced the sensory deprivation.

And looked forward to her team's arrival.

The moment after she materialized that thought, perhaps a second later or maybe hours, she had no frame of reference for time, a tightness to her being took hold.

That white-hot fire returned, singeing every nerve ending.

Instinct made her attempt to gasp for air.

And this time, her lungs filled with oxygen.

Bright red numbers flashed across her vision.

Clanging bells echoed into her ears.

She plummeted spread-eagled from the peaceful blackness.

An unforgiving hard surface smacked her entire front side, head to toe.

That hard smack, along with a loud crack, echoed into her helmet.

Then absolute blackness closed in.

Fog hazed through Celeste's mind.

Odd sensations rattled her body. Abraded over her entire backside. A vibration of sorts. That came and went, in fits and starts.

Bumping.

Dragging.

Then nothing.

But heavy breathing huffed loudly in her ears.

Followed by an animalistic grunt.

"Wake up!" growled a feminine voice. Echoing into her head. Ricocheting through her brain. A jarring impact vibrated up through the sole of her left foot. A brief flash of pain shot into the sole of her foot, up her shin, and into her knee.

Celeste swallowed hard, mouth like gritty sandpaper.

A strange flavor coated her tongue. Earthy. Metallic.

She sucked on a sore lower lip. Tasted the coppery tang of blood.

Eyelids cemented shut, she pinched them closed harder. Then popped them wide open, arching her brows and opening her mouth along with them. Immediately she squinted under an assault of blinding light.

And then she recognized the voice. "Cara?"

"Present and accounted for," Cara said. From somewhere off to her left now.

Celeste's vision cleared. But she only managed to see out the right side of her visor.

Her hand shot up to her helmet. Through the sensitive tactile fingertips of her gloves, she felt layers of something.

"Had to duct tape it," Cara said. "You cracked your noggin' open good."

"Ah." Celeste began to remember the white-hot pain, the hard fall. "Braden?"

"Slowly coming to, beside you," the commander muttered.

Celeste looked down, saw his body laid flat, his bigger boots toe-up next to hers.

"Right. 'Bout time." Cara said. "Had to drag you two lug nuts outta the drop zone. *And* our gear."

Woozy in the head still, Celeste pushed herself up into a seated position, trying to make some kind of environmental assessment through all the glaring brightness.

"Why?" Braden pushed upright as well, bending a knee. "Was the drop zone compromised?"

"Uh... yeah," Cara moved in front of the glaring light, becoming a shadowy silhouette.

"Describe." He pushed himself further up, into a squat,

13

then stood. He braced his legs wide. "In great detail."

"Ummm..." Celeste pushed up from the ground to stand and join them. Even though they both lived and breathed military, she didn't want to be dead weight dragging their team down. "Can any of you see well? It's so bright. I'm getting a splitting headache."

"What happened to you?" Braden turned toward her.

"*I* did," Cara said. "She suffered a helmet breach. Smacked down hard. Both of you did. Her worse, though. So I duct-taped her up."

He bent his helmet visor down in front of Celeste's. At the close range, his dark skin and whites of his eyes became visible. "Are you fit, soldier?"

"Yes, sir," Celeste said.

"Excellent. The hard hit might've disabled your dayshift tint. You able to pull up telemetry?"

"Telemetry," Celeste prompted her suit. An instant later, green readings flashed up. Which told her that her oxygen remained good. The environment outside habitable. The gravity near-Earth, a little on the light side. Barometric pressure twenty-nine-point-nine. Temperature a cool fifty-eight degrees. And falling. "Yeah. So far."

"Good." He gave Celeste a nod.

Then he turned back toward Cara. "Drop zone brief."

"I think it's better to see for yourself," Cara said.

Before they left, Celeste took note of only two gear cases sitting on a scrap of the pale gray deflated landing membrane, not three. Half the weaponry. And no probes. "Were we under attack?"

"Yes." Cara hiked a thumb toward their right. "In a manner of speaking."

Celeste turned toward the right, then immediately stared downward, since everything skyward blinded her.

Instead of any kind of soil, pale pinkish dust covered the environment's surface, like sugar-sand on a beach. Sparkling black rocks, pocked like Earth's pumice, littered the ground in sizes as small as golf balls on up to beach balls. An outcropping off left featured bright green boulders with crystalline surfaces. Similar to Earth's malachite.

The sky? At least at the horizon line—all she could manage to stare at for more than two seconds without a splitting headache—shone bright white.

Reflective glare from all the pink?

Tufts of plant life popped up here and there among the boulders. Most of it flat-leafed, like clover. Or spindly like some cactus. Only instead of green, the flora all bore hues of indigo and violet.

No trees, as far as she was able to see. No water, not on the surface. Not a cloud or anything similar in the monotone whiteness of the sky.

They turned and slow-walked with Cara, taking in the realm's strange surroundings. While following a shallow trail in the pink sand, from Cara dragging her passed-out teammates and gear.

All of a sudden, something dark and small buzzed through Celeste's line of vision.

But she couldn't focus on details of the flier with her right eye. And the creature zipped past her duct-taped-blind left.

Soon another small something buzzed by. Then another. Followed by two more. Then several streams of fliers sped by in one flowing current.

Blurring by, fast and level, they zoomed through the air like hummingbirds. But not one seemed interested in any of their team. Even though they all headed in their same direction.

Celeste followed close behind her crew, using their bodies to block the debilitating light.

But then, both Braden and Cara stopped cold.

Celeste almost crashed into them.

"Holy shit," Braden said under his breath.

"Exactly," Cara replied.

Celeste moved to the left of the commander. Then squinted up at a dark roiling mass in the sky. "What... *is* that?"

"Looks like they're...*feeding?*...on it?" Cara shook her head, expression dumbfounded.

"Feeding on what?" He frowned. "*What* are we looking at?"

Cara folded her arms. "Damn. And it's so much bigger than before."

From what Celeste could make out, a swirling storm of small dark shapes gyrated and reshaped. Four masses of them. Like flowing schools of fish, but upright like tornado funnels. Every now and then, smaller dark swirls would break off, dive wide or deep into some bright-colored mass about three meters above the ground, then rejoin their dark funnel once again.

"*Soldier.*" Braden turned to face Cara. "*Brief* me."

"Yes, sir." Cara angled a nod toward the roiling mass of creatures. "That orange slime. That's what they're after. We all landed face down, about the same time. But I rolled over within seconds, alert and charged."

"Adrenaline spike," he said.

"On steroids," Cara said. "But then I scrambled up from the ground. Because the white sky was freaky enough. But in a flash, out of thin air, these reddish orange blobs of slime spun to life. Right under Soteria's aperture. Then like a firehose, the slime began sealing the opening.

The more the slime sprayed itself on, the faster Soteria's opening vanished, leaving only orange slime and white sky."

"The gear?" Braden asked.

"A torn inflatable, two cases, and half the weaponry made it through," she said. "The third case got caught behind the slime."

"Probes?" he asked.

Cara shook her head. "Not a one."

Celeste blinked. "What does that mean?"

She stared at the roiling funnels of creatures that fed off the orange slime. The last of which dripped from a white sky, free of any sign of the space-time rift. No Soteria.

The knowledge came before anyone answered. They'd lost their way back home.

Correction. Wherever they'd landed... had just become home.

An inhospitable realm. So far.

Three stranded travelers. With two gear boxes between them.

"Maybe it's better not everything made it through," Celeste muttered. "If we're lucky, the homing tags will bounce the probes and case back. Alt-Realm will know something went wrong. They'll move on to a better option."

Cara frowned. "Do you think they'll attempt a rescue mission?"

"No." Braden shook his head. "And I wouldn't either. They've got millions of lives they need to save out of nine billion. Three scouts don't make a difference."

Celeste sighed. "And this planet, or realm, or alternate reality, whatever the hell it is, is defending itself. Either through biological predators or some sentience to the environment itself."

"Great." Cara planted her hands on her hips. "Now what?"

"Now we adapt, soldier." The commander put his hands at the base of his neck, released a latch, then took off his helmet.

Celeste and Cara followed suit.

Under the bright white foreign sky, eyes closed, all three of them took deep breaths of the oxygen-rich atmosphere in a brand-new world.

"Adapt, or die," Braden said.

"I vote survive." Celeste squared her shoulders, as she fought to be brave.

Tears welling in her eyes, as they began to finally adjust to the brightness, she thought of Liam.

And hoped with burning emotion her beautiful boy had a chance at a good life.

Somewhere out there. Through success of one of the other quantanaut teams.

"Let's get back to those gear cases," Celeste said, turning and staring down at their tracks in the pink sand. "And hope one of them has pairs of sunglasses."

Because she intended to do more than just survive.

In a realm where all the vital elements of Earth were present?

She intended to thrive.

And maybe, with some amount of luck and a lot of determination, they'd figure out a way to reconnect with the rest of humankind.

Where she'd be able to reunite with Liam.

Someday.

METALLIC

FROM THE SOUTH side of the world's largest domed hangar —so new, the steel arch girders gleamed under its stretch of retracted skylights—Commander Trent Jamison descended from the immense arena's upper deck.

Mood grave by the dangerous mission they were about to undertake, he took measured steps down the long concrete staircase, heading toward the departure platform.

Where their three-person quantanaut crew, Team Two, planned to leave Earth.

To arrive in another realm.

A bitter taste festered in his mouth. From the way NASA and the globe's newly formed Alt-Realm military branch had run the ramrod operation from the start.

Every step of the way, the information flow had been stymied with secrets and need-to-knows.

To protect against *whom*?

Because all nations benefited from mission success. And those same nations, every citizen of planet Earth, suffered in the worst possible way with failure.

Which meant, Alt-Realm had been keeping secrets

from the quantanauts themselves. For some idiotic reason. Because everyone's chances of success increased with knowledge.

Which Jamison planned to gain.

With or without their willing cooperation.

Yet regardless of his misgivings at that moment, Jamison proudly led his crew down. Both of his highly trained and wholly trusted teammates followed, right behind him. In all things.

Dark-gray custom state-of-the-art environmental suits clung to their bodies. Sleek revolutionary helmets hugged their skulls. An aerodynamic visor arced two inches from their noses. The suit's breakthrough design and layers of nanotech fabric supplied all the protection and monitoring needed, including oxygen reserves enough to last twelve hours.

Good thing their alternate-realm destination had breathable atmosphere.

Or they'd be shit-outta-luck in a hurry if delayed.

Yeah, his distrust of the entire operation ran deep.

Why he'd told his team—who'd backed him without question—the plans had changed. They wouldn't be entering from the sanctioned quantanaut entrance tunnel down below. Where they'd been explicitly instructed.

Because Jamison didn't take kindly to orders from scientists.

Neither did his crew.

Nor did they appreciate being lab rats tossed into a giant fishbowl. While thousands of the world's leading scientists, fanned out in a stadium-like array of workstations, gawked from above. Before preening at their own momentous achievement. Or lamenting, then covering up, some catastrophic failure.

So Jamison seized what small amount of control he could. Kept his team dedicated to the cause. Their way.

Amid a crazy-ass unrecognizable world that had begun to rapidly disintegrate. Politically. Societally.

And, in six weeks' time? Literally.

Because a planet-killer asteroid hurtled toward Earth. Damn thing measured thirty-five kilometers wide. With a direct-hit trajectory.

Flung from some god with a sense of humor. One who watched all the scrambling humans with amusement, no doubt.

That asteroid had somehow slipped beneath the radar of a polluted planet. One obsessively focused on clean energy. With activists pointing fingers at governments. And businesses racing to capitalize on sustainable energy innovation.

But too many scientists had been diverted, feverishly working on solving the planet's earth and sea problems. Not enough of them had been looking spaceward, monitoring total destruction careening toward them from the sky.

That botched responsibility ran up the flagpole though.

Too many bureaucrats focused on themselves. Instead of the bigger picture.

Of course, another more important reason fueled Jamison's decision to have their team make an unexpected entrance.

On that historic day, Team Two was the second quantanaut scouting team in as many hours. Scheduled back-to-back, among the five three-person quantanaut teams that had been training for the last five months.

All with the mission to make the leap into the vast unknown.

In search of another suitable realm.

A refuge for a doomed Earth's evacuees.

And walking in from the nosebleed section, down past dozens in high command, through the section of scientists most critical to the gateway jumps, gave Jamison a reliable bead on how things had gone on the first jump.

Knowledge. Any damn way he could get it.

And not ten steps into the thick of it, the verdict of the first jump became crystal clear: *Not good.*

Expressions ran the gamut from solemnly dour to sheer panic.

Sweat beaded across far too many brows.

All the crammed stadium bodies probably stank, that sour tang of fear.

Lips moved in animated speech.

White-smocked chests heaved with shallow breathing.

But Jamison's team, already suited, helmets engaged and tuned to a specific channel, were spared the full impact of the unfolding chaos.

Off right—within a glass-enclosed command pod that cantilevered over the stadium array of monitoring scientists —Admiral Worthington barked orders at a tight ring of five commanding officers. Face red with rage. Arms gesticulating wildly.

All wore dark-gray uniforms with black striping, but the surrounding officers sported less chest metal and lighter shoulder boards than the admiral. The larger ring beyond them, dozens of lesser officers hovering in the command pod, stood at attention in lighter gray.

Disinterested in the dressing down, Jamison's gaze pivoted, arrowing over to the jump zone at ground level. Center stage.

Soteria, their transport gateway, hovered three meters above the ground. Some strange quantum invention developed as humankind's last hope. Shaped like a figure eight. Or infinity symbol, to those prone to poetics. Opaque dark-gray: inactive.

But below the transport gateway, vibrated the cause of all the commotion.

A quarantined debris field lay scattered across the polished gray concrete, below Soteria. Something large, silvery, and square. Four smaller objects, basketball shaped.

Team One's four titanium probes? And a gear case?

All had electromagnetic shielding domes of their own. Similar to the shielding that would go up once they'd entered the drop-zone platform.

That mess meant something had gone wrong. Not everything had made it through.

"Admiral," Jamison said, tone low and calm.

A soft gasp of surprise sounded over the comm in Jamison's helmet. "Commander Jamison?" The admiral's gaze shot toward the tunnel. Then he scanned his eagle eye beneath the three-hundred-meter field stretching below Soteria. The bottom of the fish bowl. "Where are you?"

"Look left," Jamison said. He'd stopped at a wide landing halfway down.

The admiral's hulking form spun around. "You've broken protocol."

"With reason." Not that he planned to elaborate on his personal trust issues. "There's debris in our jump zone. My team will need to be fully briefed."

"You'll jump without the briefing." The admiral's tone vibrated with irritation.

"We'll be briefed," Jamison said. "Or they'll be no jump at all from my team."

Insubordination?

Absolutely.

But their specialized teams couldn't be replaced in the short time that Earth had left.

Which gifted him an incredible amount of unique leverage.

And Jamison intended to use every damn trick he knew. Planned to gain as much advantage over the unknown as possible.

When the admiral failed to respond, Jamison filled in the blanks. "We'll meet a team at the perimeter of the jump zone. I want all ten officers there: the lead scientist and head jump facilitator from every team."

"You heard the commander," Admiral Worthington barked into their comms. "Be down there before Team Two clears the stairs."

"*Yes sir!*" echoed a cacophony of replies.

Jamison resumed his descent at the same pace.

While fighting the urge to tug at the tight environmental suit at the center of his chest. And at every joint.

The latest design took some getting used to, with its heavy skin and clinginess. Made of millions of nanoscales in multitudes of layers, designed to move with the body, the suit coated his body like liquid armor. Armor that provided everything he needed to survive, even in the harshest environments. Even in space. And, when summoned, it also streamed data across his visor, about his own internal systems as well as that of whatever world existed outside the suit.

When they reached the bottom of the stairs, then strode the few steps to the entry gate, all ten men and women were waiting.

"Team One," Jamison addressed the twosome in support of the previous jump. The scientist, a tall, thin older

Swede with a shock of white hair. And the jump facilitator, a diminutive American woman with long curly red hair.

Through his helmet visor, Jamison stared at them. "Activate stress sensors," he murmured to his environmental system.

Trained to read deception, he didn't need the suit under normal circumstances. But he wanted to detect more than general deception. He wanted to know exactly which words elevated their pulses, heated their skin.

"What happened?" he prodded when neither spoke.

They looked at one another. Then the facilitator gave a nod. Carol? Or Karen, maybe. He couldn't remember.

She swallowed hard. Took a deep breath.

All while Jamison received her vital signs. Elevated pulse. Increasing blood pressure. Lowered oxygen levels. Her pale skin flushed.

"We aren't certain, Commander. But..." She took another deep breath. "It appears the Soteria's aperture sealed. On the other end."

"Sealed." Jamison wasn't sure he'd heard her correctly. That wasn't supposed to happen.

"Yes, sir," said the Swede. "The pre-jump probe had ice on it. And a reddish-orange substance."

"The team successfully made the jump?" Jamison glanced to the side. He stared at the golden quarantine shield, through to the debris field beneath.

"We believe so," said Carol/Karen.

"What makes you think the other-realm aperture sealed?" he asked.

Carol/Karen let out a heavy breath. "We haven't been able to recall them."

Them. Team One.

"Recall failure," Jamison repeated. Also deemed impossible.

Scientists had tossed some hundred thousand probes up into Soteria in the beginning months, trying to find "the other side" ... some other place to find refuge. Any other livable place. But none had come back.

Only after they'd tagged the probes with the same rare earth elements that they'd crafted Soteria with, were they able to successfully recall eighty-seven of them. And only five of those had found habitable worlds, decent oxygen, gravity, air pressure, water, and signs of life.

"But you recalled those probes?" Jamison stared at the one with the reddish orange coating. It glistened, like it had been nailed with some kind of biohazard slime.

"No." Carol/Karen shook her head. "They bounced back."

"Bounced back." Jamison let out a sigh of frustration. Parroting other's words? A new development.

"On their own. Seconds after departure," she said.

"With force," added the Swede.

Even with their elevated vital signs, both told the truth. Held nothing back. They simply didn't know.

"Clark? Stanton?" Jamison turned toward their own team's crew. A conservative French-Canadian scientist, Holly Clark, a long-haired brunette who stood almost as tall as his six-foot-three. And their ballsy jump facilitator, Gary Stanton, a salt-and-peppered crewcut who'd grown thicker in the middle over the five months of overseeing their training. "Theories?"

"We think Team One's realm grew hostile to our entry," Clark said.

"Hostile." There went the parroting again. "Like there was a sentience to the atmosphere?"

"Maybe," Clark said. Her vitals remained cooler. Calm. Like she focused on the solving the problem like the puzzle it was, nothing else.

"Stanton?" Jamison turned toward their facilitator. "Your read on it?"

The portly man shook his head. "No idea. Hostile sentient environment? Nothing we ever could've accounted for. As you know, the probes can't provide imagery. No video. No still shots. And no telemetry while in Soteria either. Only while they're on the other side."

"But we'd planned for some of that," Jamison said. Hostile lifeforms of all kinds.

And the goal all along had been to identify the best environments. Even if only one. One would work to save millions. Maybe tens of millions. Not the almost nine billion on the planet, but enough to save the human race, in hopes of seeding a fresh start somewhere else.

"We had, in a way." Stanton nodded.

No one stated the somber obvious. All three members of Team One were lost to them, if the probes could no longer get through.

Jamison's distrust in the whole damn thing kept rising.

Yet the fate of the entire world rested on their shoulders, the remaining four teams.

"Any other thoughts?" he asked, scanning the other teams' point men and women.

The willowy scientist from Team Four stepped forward. She had sleek long black hair, with thick bangs across her forehead, and bright green eyes. "The odds of a hostile environment like that happening again are minuscule."

"A million to one," agreed Team Three's ruddy brown-haired male scientist.

"A million to one," Jamison clarified, "to have aperture failure."

The scientists all looked at one another. A few murmured discussions back and forth. They then turned back toward his team, all nodding in one fashion or another.

"Stanton?" Jamison glanced at their portly jump facilitator again. "Your recommendation?"

"Make the jump. Team Two is ready. Odds, from what little information we do have, are no worse than yesterday."

"Gee thanks," Jamison said. "That's comforting." All five teams could be flying one-way tickets. To their deaths. Or trapped forever in some foreign realm.

Then again, billions of others—Earth's nonbelievers, Earth traditionalists, general non-risktakers, and any eager adventurers not lucky enough to make the evacuation cut—faced certain death.

"Team?" Jamison asked. "We a go?"

Dean Masters, the big hulking Army guy on his left gave a clipped helmet nod. "I'm *a go*, Commander."

Lorelei Woods, the lithe five-foot-six brilliant scientist on his right, bobbed her head. "Yes, sir. I'm *a go*."

"Then rev her up, Stanton," Jamison said. "We're *a go*."

Even in light of his distrust. In spite of his misgivings. And the many unknowns.

Because no one had any good choices.

But at least, Team Two had a small measure of control.

The decision to proceed. To take that leap.

To cross into the other side.

With any luck, they'd actually come back.

And be a valuable part of saving the human race.

JAMISON STOOD with his Team Two in their designated jump zone, under the massive Soteria. Hulking Masters on his left. Lithe Woods on his right.

Five minutes prior, Soteria's dark-gray figure eight had shifted translucent with activation.

Three meters above them yawned the vastness of space and time, infinite alternate universes. What he saw resembled deep space. Inky blackness. Multicolor pinpricks of light. Some bright. Others dim. The entire thing haloed in a dark blackish blue on its farthest edges.

Soteria flowed cold air around them, per the data on his visor.

But he felt snug as a bug in a rug tucked into his environmental suit.

Only detected a slight metallic scent to its oxygen-rich air.

Tasted the salt on his lips from elevated perspiration.

Because even the sturdiest of men got nervous on a first jump. Whether they were hurtling toward the ground from an airplane, or into an alternate universe through a quantum-like gateway.

A whomp of sound and vibration came from above. The colored pinpricks swirled like an oil slick on water, then spat out their pre-jump probe. The basketball-sized titanium device, plummeted, then leveled off just above the ground.

"Telemetry," Jamison said.

In response, the probe flowed data onto each of their visors.

Every data point matched the half dozen other probes they'd sent over the last two days. All the probes were tagged with identical nanotech homing beacon chips, uniquely programmed to their other-side destination. Only way they could recall the probes. And be able to replicate trips back to the same realm.

Their environmental suits were outfitted with the same place-tagged nanotech chips.

As was the pale gray inflatable positioned behind them that held three gear cases and their weaponry. Along with three new probes. All set to launch along their same trajectory, following them through the gateway.

"Check," Masters said. "Data points are clean. I'm *a go*."

"Check," said Woods. "I concur. I'm *a go*."

Jamison agreed. Even though too many things on the mission were left to chance or kept secret, his loyal team's stellar capabilities were not among them.

He hoped humankind would form a new world.

Where political bullshit got shoved aside.

"Control, we're *a go*," Jamison said, ready to depart a doomed Earth and discover a better place.

"Confirm *go* status," Admiral Worthington said.

"On our count," Jamison said.

"Three," Masters said, in his bass tone.

"Two," said Woods, cool and collected.

"One," Jamison said. Then he launched into a running start, raised his arms seventy degrees, and leapt up into Soteria at that angle. Another surprise move that broke protocol.

But he'd had a hunch. Which his team had backed.

That the trajectory they entered with had a bearing on how they landed.

And when dropping into the unknown?

They'd take any edge they could get.

As his body entered the gateway's membrane, searing pain from a million needles stabbed through his being.

Then... nothingness.

No pain. No connection to his body at all.

Total sensory deprivation. Of the physical.

But a sense of general awareness remained. A connectedness, without form or substance.

Peace and rightness washed through him.

And although he couldn't see in the traditional way, he still sensed the inky darkness and multicolored pinpricks of light. Felt one with it all.

The strong personalities of his team pressed in around him as well. The quiet but powerful strength of Masters. The vivid intellectual brightness of Woods. Both there with him. The team traveling as together one.

Left with only his mental faculties, Jamison focused on what he wanted to manifest at their destination: A smooth landing. Continuing that same arcing flight. Curling on the downward curve. Hitting solid ground in a flowing tuck-and-roll. Popping back up onto the balls of his feet, knees bent, tensed body at the ready.

Ready for anything.

Some amount of time later, seconds or minutes perhaps, the pain of a million stabbing needles returned. But he maintained a crisp focus on nailing that smooth tuck-and-roll landing.

Then he breached Soteria's membrane.

At the exact angle he'd visualized.

And on a perfectly executed tuck-and-roll, then a pop up, he stood on solid ground.

In the middle of a bizarre metallic world.

Silvery light from three moons in a diagonal line—two large on the upper left and middle, one small on bottom right, all midway up a dark night sky—glowed across a hardscape that gleamed in bright rainbow-on-silver hues.

A faint mist hung motionless in the moonlight, giving the atmosphere a glittering three-dimensional quality.

As Masters and Woods popped up beside him, in their original launch formation, they took in their immediate surroundings.

"Set to record," Jamison instructed both his visor and theirs. To date, no probe had been able to successfully bring any video or still imagery through Soteria. The scientists theorized that something within Soteria itself wiped it all. But they'd planned to capture all they could anyway. In the hopes that something would survive for further analysis later.

The glittering air swirled into small eddies around the sudden disturbance of their arrival.

Then the probes spat out right after them, all three plummeting, then hovering.

Gear cases and weaponry dropped in next, encased in the operation's launch-and-land inflatable. Like a giant pale gray beach ball, it bounced a few times before settling.

"Deflate," Jamison directed, through his suit's comm link.

The inflatable obeyed, bursting open to reveal three large silver cases, bound together with all manner of weaponry fastened into black webbing.

"Scan," Masters said.

Seconds later, illuminated in bright green on their visors, populated readings beginning at their location and radiating toward the horizon in every direction. All the information matched what their pre-jump probe had reported. And those half dozen probes before that.

"Life signs," said Woods.

At that request, all they got was a blue light with dashes

instead of data. "Inconclusive," said a monotone low female AI voice over their comm link.

"What the hell does that mean?" grumbled Masters, walking toward their gear.

"Something out there is *half* alive?" Jamison guessed.

Woods sighed. The biologist among them, she loved when they interjected their inexpert two cents. "It *means* that our definition of 'life' might not apply here. Biologically speaking, there might be elements indicative of life, but not in the same way our Earth-bound parameters recognize."

Masters examined the bundle of cases, then began freeing weapons from the webbing. "It's either 'alive' or it isn't."

"What you really mean is: it's either a 'threat or not.'" Woods caught the hefty laser rifle that Masters tossed her way.

"Now, children." Jamison strode between them and unfastened his own rifle. "How 'bout we don't fight with each other just yet. Save your energy to ensure this new place decides to be nice and friendly. Let's assume *everything* is alive. And a threat. Until proven otherwise."

"Spoken like true soldiers," Woods grumbled.

"Through and through," Masters said.

"Onward." Jamison directed, knowing their bluster carried an affectionate undertone. And had a calming effect, especially in the unsettling circumstances.

"Track point," Masters said, marking their position on a modeling map grid.

"Direction?" Woods asked.

The metallic terrain varied. Some elevations stretched flat toward the horizon, speckled with circular depressions. A portion of the nearby terrain rose in jagged steep black spires, anywhere from seven to thirty meters high. Faint dark silhouettes, along half the horizon lines, suggested larger mountains.

They had almost two-hundred-seventy degrees of flat to choose from.

But high ground would give them a broader view.

Jamison surveyed the spires, then slung his rifle strap over his chest, spinning the weapon onto his back. "Anyone up for climbing?"

"I'm game," Woods said, slinging her rifle onto her back in the same manner. Scientist or not, they'd all been extensively trained in a multitude of areas. And the lithe woman had excelled in climbing.

"You know it," Masters said, following suit. Then he popped open one of their cases and retrieved climbing gear.

Ten minutes later, they were ascending the smoothest face of the thirty-meter spire. Masters took lead, Woods center, and Jamison pulled up the rear.

Clanks sounded as Masters hammered steel pins into place. Clicks followed as they connected their carabineers to ropes. No free-climbing allowed. No risk-taking that jeopardized the mission goal: identify a viable refuge.

The spire, made of a dense black granite, covered in fine metallic dust according to their readings, made for stable climbing. Weathered dull, striated with surface cracks, rough and irregular yet solid beneath, the rock made for smooth climbing.

Halfway up, Jamison paused. "Hold position." He spun in his harness to survey from their vantage.

"Zoom twice," Jamison instructed his visor, activating the built-in binoculars, focusing on what appeared to be some sort of shadowy movement. "Zoom, again."

Multiple large objects moved. Slow. But definite movement. Big and dark. Gray, maybe.

"You getting this, Woods?" Jamison asked.

"Got it," she said. "Life signs?" she repeated, cueing up data.

Blue-lit dashes flashed across his visor again. "Inconclusive," droned their ever-helpful AI.

"So, inconclusive means alive. Noted," Masters said.

"Threat?" Jamison asked.

"Uncertain," Woods said. "Too far away to tell."

"How many do you count?" He spotted two dozen or so distinct moving shadows.

"Thirty... forty, maybe," she said. "Looks like a herd of tuskless elephants."

"Well, high ground seems safe." From whatever those things were.

"Targeting a drone toward them to investigate," she said.

"Uh... Commander?" Masters said. "Zero in on your two o'clock. What the hell is *that*?"

Jamison focused to his slight right.

Under the bright triple moonlight, a glimmering gigantic mass headed their way.

Fast.

"Zoom," Jamison directed his visor binocs. Rippling occurred greatest at the glimmering mass's edges. And those edges and the entire form undulated, morphing in both dimension and shape. "Looks like a school of fish."

"Or a swarm of locusts," Woods murmured.

At an invisible directional line, where the silvery locusts bisected between Team Two's location and the elephant shadows, the shifting mass split into two. About a third of it veered off, heading toward the shadow herd. The larger portion banked, arrowing directly toward them.

"That's not coincidence," Masters said.

"An assault team for foreigners?" Jamison spun his rifle around front. At their rate of speed, they had less than a minute before the mass entered firing range.

"Attracted to what?" Woods asked. "Our drone isn't a life form. So why the drone?"

"Maybe the shadow-beast herd," Jamison guessed. Those beasts, no matter what they were made of, were life forms. Even if inconclusive ones.

"Maybe..." Woods stared off toward her tuskless elephants. "Zoom, five times."

"Estimated time of arrival here?" Jamison asked.

"Twenty-five seconds," Masters said.

"And there?" Jamison asked.

"Eighteen." Masters pulled his weapon forward as well.

"Do you have telemetry from the herd probe?" Jamison asked.

"Yes," Woods said. "The probe is over the herd now."

"Are the shadow-beasts reacting to the drone?" Any information better prepared them.

"Negative," Woods said.

"Are they reacting to anything at all? To the locust swarm?"

She gave a slight headshake. "Negative."

"The question is, are they aiming for the herd?" Jamison thought aloud. "Or the drone?"

The moons had begun to set. The smallest already sunk under the horizon, the middle-large about halfway down.

Jamison did a scan of the rest of the horizon, surveying further to ensure they were ready for anything. Even an attack on multiple fronts.

An orange hue lit up the horizon opposite to the setting moons. Perhaps the realm's sun about to rise.

"Report," Jamison said, swinging his gaze back around.

"Five..." Masters stared intently at the shadow herd. "four... three... two... and contact."

"Seven seconds on our end," Jamison said.

"The locusts are chasing the drone," Woods confirmed.

"And the drone?" he asked.

"Zipping the hell out of there," Woods said. "With the swarm giving chase."

"Four..." Masters called a new countdown.

The silvery mass arrowing their way brightened, then darkened.

"Three..." Woods continued, swinging her rifle around.

Then the glimmers illuminated again, flashing a brilliant whitish silver. As if the individuals in that flying swarm were electrified.

"Two..." Masters murmured.

Each of them took a deep breath, as trained when beginning an assault. Or a defense.

"Contact," Jamison muttered, when the creatures breached the hundred-meter line.

Right as the mass's individual forms became distinguishable from their larger group. They resembled flying sideways jellyfish. Round on front. A fat ring behind. Then multiple trailing tentacles. Their bodies shimmered with electrified iridescence, similar in color to the metallic iridescence coating the ground surface and spires.

The flying school dove toward them, straight on.

"Commander?" Masters asked. "What are our orders with these aggressive jellyfish?"

"Fire at will," Jamison said.

And they did. As a unit, the three fired their laser rifles on rapid burst.

Which sizzled and dropped the leading jellyfish fliers.

Only to be replaced by those zooming in from behind.

"They're coming around," Masters said, turning left, firing on a new splintered attack.

"Got 'em on my side," said Woods, turning right, firing toward her flanking maneuver.

Then a realization hit Jamison like a lightning bolt as he fired at the attackers.

What the drone and their team had in common.

"Kill the drone," Jamison ordered.

"Sir?" Woods said, while continually firing.

"Shut down the herd drone. I have a hunch. Want to confirm."

"Yes sir!" Woods continued firing at her stream, dropping jellyfish like zapped flies, all while deactivating the drone she'd programmed. "...probe 5743, commence immediate shutdown."

Jamison couldn't shake his middle section of jellyfish fliers, which streamed ten times as thick as their flanking offshoots. "Can anyone get a bead on the drone's school?"

"Gimme a sec," Masters said. "That school... it's... diverting."

"Away from the drone?" Jamison asked.

"Yes. Not toward us, either. Those jellyfish did a one-eighty, heading back to wherever they came from." A sudden gasp sounded. "*Ackch!*" Masters swore under his breath. "I'm hit. One of those damn tentacles zapped me."

"Where?" Woods asked, the most experienced medic among them.

"Left thigh," Masters grumbled with a lisp. As if speaking through clenched teeth.

"You fit to continue fighting?" Jamison asked.

"Think so." Masters growled. The pissed off guy shot a more aggressive barrage of laser bursts into the never-ending attack. "Just burns like a mother."

"Everyone trust my hunches?" Jamison asked, tone calm and cool.

"Yes, sir!" They shouted, in unison.

"Shut it all down," Jamison said. "All of us. Everything. At the exact same time. The shooting. And our environmental suits. Full shutdown."

"Sir?" Woods asked. "We won't be able to breathe."

"Disengage your helmet," he said. The atmosphere would be breathable. Even if they didn't yet know on a microscopic level what they'd be exposing themselves to. "But only if you need to."

"Understood," she said.

"Give the laser bursts all you've got to buy a few seconds of lead time," he said. "And on my mark."

"Three..." Jamison took a deep breath.

While they amplified their laser bursts at the onslaught.

"Two..." Jamison increased his laser spray, widening the spread back and forth to catch any clever ones seeking to break through.

"One..." he said, hoping he'd guessed right.

"*Shutdown*," they all said simultaneously, powering everything down, suits and weapons.

Their visors went dark.

Weapons fell cold.

And for a heartbeat's time, the creatures paused, a vibration rippling through their ranks.

An instant later, the swarm blossomed outward, flying wide. As if the swarm hit an invisible solid wall ahead of Team Two, then flowed outward and away, along that barrier.

Jamison held his breath. Counting the seconds. While he watched the swarm fly back, heading toward where the mass had come from.

He counted past ten...

The silvery glimmer grew smaller, shadowed with distance and the setting third moon.

He counted past twenty...

They'd trained heavily for this type of circumstance.

Even with adrenaline pumping through their veins.

Yet nothing prepared the body quite like the real deal.

Soon his lungs began to scream for oxygen.

Exhaling a little helped with that desperate instinctive sensation. "Hold," he reminded the others. If they could. As long as they dared, without risking blackout.

"Hold..." Woods replied. The word they'd been trained to use with a slow exhale.

"Hold..." Masters said, joining in.

"Hold..." they all said together, dangled from their ropes halfway down the jagged spire.

"*Hold...*" all again. "For just *one more* time..." Jamison added.

"*Hold...*"

That was all they could handle.

"Activate Team Two suits," Jamison ordered.

Oxygen flooded back into their helmets. And the sounds of sucking, their collective dragging in deep lungfuls of air, gasped across their comms.

But the swarm never veered off its return course. Continued the new trajectory, away from them.

After a good minute or two of silent reoxygenating, Woods chimed in. "It was the vibrations. The drone and us. They reacted to our vibrations. Maybe because both were in play."

"Maybe they detected our tie to the drone," Jamison said. "Which could've amplified the outward vibration that attracted them in the first place."

"And now?" Masters asked.

"We should cut that drone loose. Call it a loss." Wasn't worth the danger.

"What now." Masters let out a heavy sigh. "To the top?"

"No." Jamison stared at a near-blinding sunrise. "I think we're done here."

"We are?" Woods asked, surprise clear in her tone.

"Yeah." Jamison nodded toward the red globe burning just above the horizon. Small compared to Earth's sun. Surrounded by deep black, because of its greater distance.

Yet all of the preliminary probes had given acceptable temperature surface readings. Which meant that rising sun burned hotter. From farther away. Something Earth had no way of detecting without video or imagery. A fact only Team Two were able to ascertain.

"Oh. That's not good," Woods said.

"No," Masters agreed. "We *are* done here."

Because the metallic realm they'd landed on had a dying sun. At some advanced stage of decay. Which meant humans wouldn't have long in the metallic realm either. Months. Years. Decades. Even centuries. But certain extinction on the near-term, if their species colonized there.

"This place will never be a refuge for us," Jamison said.

"Good," Masters said. "I don't want to live in a world with swarming jellyfish."

"Last one down's a rotten egg!" Woods called, releasing her rope, zipping down past him.

Then he and Masters raced each other to the ground.

THREE HOURS LATER, Team Two time, they landed back into the jump zone.

Which ended up being three days later, Earth-time.

Their video, imagery, and audio all came back blank.

The admiral himself met them down on ground level.

"Admiral Worthington." Jamison gave the man a slow nod of respect, weary from the ordeal of traveling through the gateway twice, and the tense battle in between. "Team Two world is a no go."

The admiral frowned. Deeply. "Are you certain?"

"Yes," Jamison said. "It's begun the slow death of getting fried by its sun."

"Very well." Worthington gave them a curt nod. "You're all dismissed for the day. Hit decontamination, then cool off. I'll expect you back at oh-five-hundred for duty."

"Yes, sir," Jamison said.

Then they all headed toward that tunnel they'd been instructed to take. Jamison was too tired to be ornery about it. A fresh dose of distrusting defiance could wait till morning.

"Sir?" He glanced back toward the admiral, brows raised. "The other teams?"

"None have returned yet, son." His voice softened. "You're the first."

Jamison sighed. "They'll be back."

They had to be. The human race counted on those other last teams, exploring their three realms. One of them had to be suitable.

"Well, crew," Jamison said, roping an arm around both of their shoulders, Masters on his left, Woods on his right. "Let's go hose off, then grab some beers. First round's on me."

"I'm buying our second." Masters let out a heavy sigh.

"I've got the third." Woods gave a decided nod.

Because they were celebrating.

Team Two hadn't discovered Earth's refuge.

But they had prevented an even worse disaster.

They'd crossed one destination off Earth's list.

A metallic ticking time bomb.

Jamison shot out a fervent hope, that the other teams hit pay dirt.

EMBRYONIC

Stark terror bled into the confidence Tasha Blane had worked so hard to gain.

A pounding heart battered the inside of her ribcage.

Shallowed breaths stuttered, reduced to ragged gasps.

Fragments of worry and fear spun out of control.

Team Three, her and two teammates—both not only highly trained quantanauts, but unlike her, career military—exited the long concrete tunnel and began the last strides of their march into a cavernous stadium-like military hangar. Constructed of steel so new it gleamed. Incorporating some top-secret rare earth elements, giving the steel a darker blackish blue sparkle.

The sides of the monstrous hangar arced up toward retractable skylights running down its center, opened to gather midday light. Concrete risers spanned up and all around, the stadium accommodating thousands of the world's leading scientists at individual workstations. The White Coats were all heads-bent, captivated by their data tablets. Together, a daunting array of minds and technology, making the mission—one she'd been both anticipating and dreading—possible.

A *military* mission.

For meek microbiologist her.

Her temperament had always been best suited to quiet labs, dependable microscopes, and single cell organisms. Where she maintained control. When she remained queen of her universe.

Not as some helpless gladiator, thrown to the lions, forced to fight or die.

Mental melodramatics do nothing to help you, Tasha.

Wise words from her twice-weekly therapist.

She sucked in a deeper breath, grateful for the clingy barrier of the state-of-the-art environmental suit her keepers had outfitted her with. Dark gray and fashioned from multiple layers of nanotech woven into the fabric, its protection also kept her separate from the chaos. Like a cocooning security blanket. Custom designed specifically for the mission. Complete with sleek head-hugging helmet. Which had a nifty visor with a slight smoky tint that hovered close to her skin, like full-face sunglasses.

"Music," she murmured.

A beat later, her favorite playlist began to stream. Thumping rock music. One of many anchors that helped to ground her. Since the rest of the world kept spiraling away from reality.

Van Halen's "Best of Both Worlds" pulsed into her ears.

Cool ionized air flowed through her nostrils.

And the sweet berry taste of a dissolving elderberry lozenge floated over her tongue.

The hard lozenge had become another anchor that day. From the fourth bag she'd bought. *After* she'd fully recovered from a cold.

Because... *Normal.* Throat lozenges. And common colds. And rock music.

In the last weeks, as the deadline neared, she'd needed more of any normal she could get.

The remaining half of that lozenge bag bulged in her right thigh pocket. Not that she could pop another right away. Not fully helmeted. But it helped calm her to know they were there. For later.

Mental-focus tools got her to put one foot in front of the other. Take things one step at a time. Through a mission she'd never imagined being a part of six short months ago.

Like concentrating on the dark-gray swath of fabric between Commander Branson Trebec's broad shoulders ahead of her, as her team approached the quantum jump zone. And maintaining peripheral awareness to her immediate right of their third teammate, Kellie Langstad.

Not on the stadium filled with thousands of scientists.

Not on the world falling apart outside the hangar.

Definitely not the daunting realm-jumping phenomenon. That her team was about to leap through. For the very first time.

NASA, along with the newly formed Alt-Realm branch of the military, had constructed the behemoth hangar for a very specific purpose.

To house the gigantic quantum phenomenon that they'd constructed within it.

Soteria.

Gateway to infinite alternate realms.

Named after the goddess of salvation and deliverance. To inspire hope.

Hope.

Another mental anchor to help crutch her through the next few minutes.

Because they'd stopped walking. Had taken position in the jump zone. In the center of the arena. Directly beneath Soteria.

The massive invention hovered three meters above the concrete floor in powerful silence. Spanning three-hundred meters long and half as wide, shaped like an infinity symbol, the dark-gray tubular structure had been made with a unique combination of those rare earth elements.

In order to save a doomed Earth.

From the planet-killer asteroid delightfully named Thanatos. Deliverer of Death.

Nothing like frightening dramatics on every headline. Every damn day.

No wonder why she needed therapy. And physical anchors. And mental coping tools.

Time till impact? Till the end of all life on Earth?

Six minuscule weeks.

The blink of an eye. A footnote in Earth's history.

Which made her panic-attack? Ridiculous.

Better to die braving new worlds. Finding alternate possibilities. A refuge for humankind. Than wait around to get crushed, exploded, or broiled to death.

After exhaling a slow breath, she sucked harder on the last remnants of the elderberry lozenge on her tongue. She'd burned through three bags of them surviving that nasty cold she'd gotten. Worn down. From the stress of everything outside. And with all the unsettling things she'd learned on the inside.

Breathe, Tasha. *You're alive. You're safe.*

A mantra she'd been telling herself over the last five months. After her recruitment. During their intensive and unrelenting training.

Her soothing rock music cut out abruptly.

"Commence jump sequence," ordered Admiral Worthington.

Jump sequence. Not *launch*. A semantics difference deemed important to the skittish non-military members. They were rocket-less after all. Only environmental suits protected them from whatever harsh forces of space and time they might face on their journey.

Because no one truly knew.

Scientists had purportedly tossed tens of thousands of probes up into the gateway. Later, after months of failure, wisely tagged with unique homing chips made of the same rare earth elements cocktail as Soteria.

Only eighty-seven returned. Because their destinations hadn't destroyed them (according to theorists.)

Of those, only five were goldilocks realms, having the elements necessary to sustain life.

But not one probe had been able to bring back viable imagery, no still photos, no video.

No audio, either.

Which meant *something* within the transport nullified certain kinds of technology. Affected the probes. Only enabled analog data to remain. From rudimentary instruments.

What kind of effect did Soteria have on humans?

Inconclusive.

Quantanauts had become humankind's guinea pigs.

Aside from the brave souls who had gone before them to test Soteria itself. But not to the five goldilocks worlds, apparently.

The results of the very first explorations?

The Genesis Team?

Classified.

Right. Didn't exactly give off warm-fuzzy vibes.

Unable to keep focus on her anchors, she swallowed the disintegrating remains of her elderberry lozenge.

She shot a glance toward the command platform, from where Admiral Worthington had given the order. The cantilevered structure jutted farther out past the stadium workstations of the scientists, seemingly perched in the air above them.

With a whomping vibration, Soteria activated.

Refusing to look up, not till she absolutely had to, she caught the dark-gray membrane of the massive tubular infinity structure that hovered above them fading, going translucent.

Instead, she focused on the sudden movement of their jump facilitator, Greer Patterson.

And did her best to ignore several glittering electrical quarantine shields, which had been netted over unidentifiable objects on the concrete floor of the jump zone beyond him.

Patterson strode from the perimeter into her line of sight, wearing tan chinos and a white dress shirt, no tie, two buttons undone, sleeves rolled. He clutched their pre-jump probe, a basketball-sized device made of titanium, tightly in his hands. Large of frame, with a ruddy complexion and brown hair tending toward a slight curl, he huffed just from the half dozen steps with the added heft of the probe.

After positioning himself a few meters ahead of their team, he stopped and looked up. He squatted slightly, bounced twice in place, arms and knees bending with the motion, then tossed the probe up into Soteria.

Once the ball sailed within a half meter of Soteria's invisible membrane, the probe got sucked up, disappearing from sight.

Warning bells clanged into Tasha's ears.

A calm deep female AI voice issued a warning. Her oxygen levels had dipped.

Probably because she'd forgotten to breathe.

Commander Trebec spun around at the warning.

Langstad crowded in from the right.

Because they'd also received the warnings about their struggling teammate.

The two of them bowed their helmets down, till all three helmet visors touched.

Close enough to dissipate the glare from the brightness of the stadium, allowing Tasha to see the whites of their eyes, the furrows of their brows, concern evident in their expressions.

She swallowed hard, then exhaled. "I'm good."

Having observed her survivable panic attacks before, they knew the demons she faced. They even insisted on helping her work through them. And in keeping her as a valued member of their team.

"You got this." Trebec clapped her on the shoulder.

"*We* got this," Langstad said. Then she lifted a gloved finger to the visored space in front of her lips. "Shhh... Don't tell anyone. But I'm scared shitless."

"Me too." Trebec gave her shoulder a light squeeze. "But don't tell anyone."

They'd all just told plenty of people. Their comm channel reached the ten people who were frontline support staff to the teams, all five teams' scientists and jump facilitators. Along with the admiral and the entire command center.

Tasha quirked up a half smile. "Not very commanderly?"

He snorted. "As if I give a rat's ass what any White Coats think."

"We *got* this," Langstad repeated. She lifted her helmet an inch, then clunked it back down onto theirs, a gentle helmet bump. "No time to be scared. Or even think about ourselves. Concentrate. Act. Complete the mission. We're gonna save the world. *We* go. *They* go."

First, the five teams. To find a suitable realm. A refuge for humankind.

For the lucky millions able to make the leap. Among those willing to forsake the only world they'd ever known, to risk survival in another. As opposed to the whole crushed, exploded, broiled alternative.

Tasha let out a slow exhale. "Concentrate. Act. Complete the mission."

Things to focus on.

With a team that had her back.

After another resonating whomp, the pre-jump probe dropped out from Soteria.

But not one of them broke their stabilizing huddle.

No need. The probe's telemetry populated on their visors. Providing data of the realm they were about to jump into.

And every reading matched the half dozen probes sent to their location over the last two days. All remained stable, within tolerable ranges. Atmosphere, pressure, gravity, temperature.

"Do this together?" Commander Trebec glanced at Tasha, then Langstad as he clamped his other gloved hand onto her teammate's shoulder.

"Yep," Langstad said, clamping a hand onto each of their shoulders. "Like skydiving. Nuthin' to it."

"Yeah." Tasha landed her gloved hands onto their shoulders too. "I'm *a go.*"

"I'm *a go.*"

"Stanton," Trebec said. "Confirming *go* status."

"Go status, acknowledged," Stanton replied.

"On our countdown," Trebec reminded them.

The sequence they'd drilled dozens of times.

"Three." Langstad gave a clipped nod.

"Two." Tasha sucked in a deep breath of air.

"One," Trebec said. "And... *go.*"

As a team, they squatted, then burst upward, everyone extending their arms at the last minute to gain maximum height. To reach into that last-half-meter zone, where Soteria engages with the jumpers, pulling them in.

And at that last split second, Tasha finally stared upward.

Vastness beyond her wildest imaginings yawned.

Breathtaking beauty sparkled back, pinpricks of light in a multitude of colors.

Depth and dimension, time and space, everything in existence.

A flash of searing pain ignited every nerve ending as she breached Soteria's membrane.

And then...

Absolute nothingness.

No, Tasha thought.

Not absolute *nothingness.*

More like... pure awareness. And nothing else.

Not the extraneousness of sensory perception.

No pain. Not physically or psychologically.

Not the slightest connection to her body... or her fears.

Soteria had swallowed her whole. And in doing so, had somehow incorporated her as an important thread in the fabric of the universe. No idea how she knew that. She simply did.

Not just her. The entire team.

They had become a part of not only the vastness, but one another.

For Trebec and Langstad pressed in, around, and through her. A vital part of her essence. And combined, their essences existed as a part of everything. Where had their physical forms gone? No idea.

Fragments of random thoughts drifted in and out of her mind, like dandelion tufts sailing along a gentle breeze. Neutral concepts, neither good nor bad. Mission parameters. Plans that had been programed. Knowledge that secrets had been kept from them by Alt-Realm. Solid trust, only in the one thing they could control: their thoughts and actions at any given moment.

Whatever phenomenon she traveled through, the strange quasi-nothingness, it magnified the concepts she'd been striving toward. Strength of mind. Peace amid chaos.

Like none of the little things mattered.

Only the greater whole.

Represented as one step at a time.

Nothing else.

Purity in adapting to whatever the path brings.

Every time her worries or anxieties fought to coalesce... *What happened to her body? Had she somehow disassembled? Would she be reassembled without harm? Where would they land? Would they discover a viable realm? Would they survive it?* ...a flood tide of tranquility surged around her, inundating the negative emotion, before washing it out into the vast nothingness sea.

At some point later, seconds or minutes, maybe longer (she had no frame of reference), searing pain flashed. Every damn nerve ending of a *very physical* body lit up as if she'd been thrust into a three-thousand-degree forge.

And then...

She shot down out of the nothingness into a greenish dimly lit somethingness.

Warning bells clanged into her ears.

Bright red lights flashed across her visor.

A calm female AI voice warned, "Oxygen critically low."

And with a gasp of air, she sucked in the cool ionized air inside her helmet.

Right as a dark rocky surface rushed toward her face.

In the split second before crash landing, Tasha somehow did an instinctive whole-body flinch, leading with her left shoulder.

Which began to flip her over.

Then she smacked down onto the very solid ground, shoulder first.

A low grunt rumbled from her throat at the sudden hard impact.

Her head spun, as that slightest left-rotation tumbled her sideways. With great force.

Which struck her as strange... once she'd settled to a stop some half-dozen spins later.

Because the realm purportedly had similar pressure, atmosphere, and gravity as Earth, according to the probes. Yet physical reactions to minuscule movements seemed... amplified.

That clanging alarm bell, the helmet's low-oxygen

warnings, cycled off as she deeply inhaled her environmental suit's oxygen.

A familiar sweet scent laced the charged air, almost like cotton candy. Residual from the elderberry lozenge... mixed with ionized air?

Resting on her belly, she lifted her head and propped up onto her elbows, in time to catch the others crash down into similar tumbling landings.

Onto a dark blackish brown surface. Rough terrain. Rocky and devoid of any signs of plant life. Like they'd landed onto some volcanic moon.

Soteria's departure point hovered larger than life above them. Inky black, with its pinpricks of colored lights that moved with great dimension, corkscrewing into a gentle swirl.

A nighttime sky framed the gateway, a softer deep black, speckled with winking silvery stars.

Then from Soteria's membrane, spat out their three scheduled mission probes. All three plummeted as a group to just above the ground, then hovered.

A giant pale gray ball dropped out next, the operation's launch-and-land inflatable that contained their gear and weaponry. With greater speed, it came down at a slight angle, bounced once, then again, before rolling away from them, across dark-brown rocky terrain.

"Deflate!" Tasha shouted through her suit's comm link, pushing up off the ground.

The inflatable instantly obeyed, bursting open.

But with its momentum, the opened ball wobbled, tangled into its inflatable, then thumping-rolled twice more before stopping.

While all three of them gave chase to the thing for a good hundred meters.

"Let's roll it backwards, to untangle it," said Trebec. "We're not going anywhere unarmed."

Tasha took the near corner of the large two-cubic-meter bundle. Langstad the middle.

Trebec took hold of the opposite corner with both hands, using his greater strength to guide the roll. He grunted, using more force and leverage than the rest of them.

Once they righted the bundle enough to expose its three silver hard cases, bound by webbing with various weapons strategically strapped into place, Tasha and Langstad began to unfasten their laser pistols and rifles.

When Langstad handed Trebec his weapons, he holstered the pistol at his hip, then slung the rifle over his back. While they armed themselves, he pulled back, surveying their surroundings. "Scan."

Bright green data illuminated across their visors. Readings that their suits picked up from their point out, toward every horizon.

Most of the data matched the pre-jump probe. And the six probes in the two days prior. But... not all.

The atmospheric readings had altered slightly.

Less oxygen.

More of some other element.

"Tropospheric composition." Tasha needed to drill down, discover why the difference. And science remained her domain on the mission. No matter the discipline. Because even though valued for her biologic expertise, they'd all been cross-trained in various areas. Her mostly in all sciences. Chemistry. Geology. Meteorology.

They'd even trained timid microbiologist her in battle tactics and war strategy.

Go figure.

Green data populated with the realm's gas mixture at the surface, mostly nitrogen and oxygen. Along with minute amounts of other gases, argon, krypton, helium, methane, neon, and hydrogen.

But then a blue light flashed across their visors.

"Well, that's a new color," Trebec muttered.

"Unknown element," the female AI voice droned. "displacing oxygen."

"We need to move," Tasha said. "Scan. Look for areas of higher oxygen content."

"The gear cases?" Langstad asked.

"Leave 'em." Trebec gave a hard headshake. "Alive first. Equipped later."

"Ideal oxygen located," the AI voice purred. "Bearing twelve degrees. Distance three hundred twenty meters."

"Let's check it out," Trebec said.

He led them in the identified direction, using their visors' topographical mapping system as their guide.

Because the primary mission remained a scouting one.

Each of the five teams had been assigned a destination realm. Each team's mission? Verify the viability of their realm as a refuge.

And for a viable realm, humans needed the correct breathable oxygen mix.

As they strode across the dark barren landscape at a brisk clip, something about their surroundings disturbed her. But she couldn't quite place the reason. Instinct? Or fear of the unknown? She couldn't tell the difference.

"In case any of you are wondering? My helmet stays on." She punched her tone with force. Which soothed her frazzled nerves. Because even though protocol dictated their remaining fully suited, including helmets, it felt good to take a stand on that.

"Noted," Trebec said. "And seconded. Mine stays the hell on too."

"Thirded." Langstad gave a hard nod. "This place gives me the creeps."

The rocky landscape continued as far as she could see.

They'd covered most of their distance within a handful of minutes.

"Scan tropospheric composition." Maybe they'd gotten close to the perimeter.

Blue light flashed again. "Unknown element," purred Little Miss AI again. "Displacing oxygen."

"Estimated Time of Arrival?" Trebec asked.

"Unknown." Came the reply.

Seconds later, warning bells clanged into their helmets.

"Warning," Little Miss AI said, "unknown threat approaching. With speed."

They all stopped and scanned the terrain in different directions.

"Nature of threat?" Langstad excelled in battle strategy.

"Unknown," the AI replied.

"Location?" Langstad asked.

"Indeterminate," the AI said.

Trebec sighed, while he and Langstad continued to scan the horizon line.

The hairs stood up on the back of Tasha's neck. She glanced over her shoulder, getting the eerie sense they were being watched.

Flowing over the terrain like a rushing tsunami, bright green *fog?* raced their way.

"Behind us!" Tasha shouted. "Run!"

To the others' credit, they didn't waste time turning around. They just launched ahead with her, sprinting full force. Trusting her implicitly.

"Describe it." Langstad pulled out ahead of them, in the lead.

"Looked like fog," Tasha replied. "But it's a weird bright green color."

"Wide and tall?" Trebec asked, "like a haboob?"

"No. Wide," Tasha replied, huffing from exertion. "But not tall. Low to the ground. About three meters high."

"Langstad, you see what I see?" Trebec asked, finally sounding a little winded.

"You bet your ass I do," Langstad said. "Off right, everyone. Up as high and as fast as we can. Let's hope whatever the hell that bright green weirdness is can't climb."

Off right, dark steep spires, some ten meters in diameter, jutted up from the ground. But as Team Three approached, additional features of the spires became apparent. Less steep toward the bottom. Gaping round holes along the surfaces, like molten rock which had cooled.

With running leaps, each of them landed on the base of the same nearest tall spire, side by side, and began race-climbing upward.

Tasha scrambled up. Toes of her boots scraping the angled face. Gloved fingers clawing and scrambling for purchase as she climbed ever higher.

"Altitude?" Trebec asked.

"Four meters," said the AI.

"Higher," Langstad voted.

"Seconded," Tasha said. The freaky green fog, whatever it was, gave her the heebie-jeebies.

"Thirded," Trebec said.

All for one. One for all.

Heart pounding, gasping for breath, Tasha finally stopped climbing when they ran out of real estate to climb without technical climbing gear.

Clinging to the side of the spire, they finally looked down and across the landscape.

Bright green fog flooded across the whole valley floor. Dark mountain ranges surrounded the valley, their ridge-lines silhouetted against a starry sky.

But farther back from where they'd come from?

Beyond the flowing green fog, up in the night sky above the slivered opening of Soteria, hung a giant gold-ringed planet. Illuminated by a moon that had begun to rise over a distant mountain range.

"Whoa," Tasha said.

The green fog appeared to splash against the bottom of their spire, then flowed some distance higher. Maybe some-thing to do with that strange overreaction-to-motion phenomenon. But even though a few tendrils spiraled upward, a good meter remained between them and the bizarre fog.

"Phew." Relief slumped Tasha's shoulders.

"Now what?" Trebec asked.

"Tropospheric composition," Tasha said.

"Unknown elements present," the AI purred.

"Hmmm..." Tasha's thoughts began tumbling as she watched how the gas acted.

"Theories," Trebec prompted. Because he knew how her mind worked. Had teased her mental processes out multiple times.

"The gas, or whatever it is, seems to be dissipating," she said, watching it thin at the edges after the force of the initial tide. "Like a giant pressure cooker got released."

"Anything similar on Earth?" Langstad asked.

"Volcanic eruptions," Tasha said. "Of all kinds. Volca-noes. Geysers. Vents. Hot springs. They are a planet's pres-sure release system."

"With green gas like that?" Trebec asked.

"Volcanoes sometimes release a chlorine gas," Tasha said. "Not sure if it's the same. But if our readings are coming back as an unknown element, it's got something unique we haven't yet been exposed to or identified."

"You both good to hang up here a while?" Trebec asked.

"I'm good," Langstad said.

"Yup," Tasha agreed.

Didn't matter if they had state-of-the-art environmental suits by Earth standards. If that unknown substance had caustic properties and ate through their suits? They were toast. Very burnt toast.

Hours later, the majority of the fog dissipated enough for them to climb down from their perch. They'd spent the time up on the spire running mental drills. Quizzing one another about military procedures, warfare tactics, and medical triage situations.

And all of the rapid-fire brain teasers had distracted Tasha enough that she hadn't longed for any of her anchors. Not even her elderberry lozenges.

By the time they climbed down, the green gas had settled into glowing steamy pools in low depressions all over the terrain. "Don't get too close to those," she warned.

They walked single file on narrow strips of higher ground between the steaming depressions.

"Not planning on it." Langstad snorted, then gave a hard headshake.

Tasha swore the terrain had been more level as they sprinted than it seemed with those low-lying gaseous pools. But then, they had been running faster than she'd ever run before. Good thing she hadn't tripped on any of the depressions.

"So what's the verdict?" Trebec asked. "We have about six more hours, if we need them. Want to explore more?"

"Hell no." Langstad snorted again, then crossed her arms. "We barely escaped that weirdness."

"No." Still uneasy about the environment, she agreed. Even though disappointment weighted heavy in her chest. "We got separated from our way out." Away from Soteria. And their gear and the probes. "If that is pressure releasing, it might not happen again for a while. But if it's something else?" She shrugged. "Who knows."

"I won't risk losing our ticket home." Trebec glanced up at Soteria. "It's decided, then. We go back."

"We go back," she and Langstad said, in near unison.

Because with all the unknowns, with the elements present and regarding the odd physics that the world exhibited with force and motion, their scouted realm proved too risky to colonize. They could be sentencing Earth's refugees to an even greater death than by Thanatos's fiery threat.

A great sense of pride bloomed in Tasha's chest.

That she'd conquered her fears and faced the great unknown.

Had Team Three accomplished their mission?

Not in the way she'd hoped. But they had explored. Had seen enough. Plenty to rule out a too-volatile embryonic realm. Because if volcanic, humankind would be jumping out of the line of fire and onto a potential volcano waiting to blow.

But an enormous layer of confidence had strengthened her foundation.

She could leap into the unknown. With a trusted team who had her back.

More importantly, she now knew... she could trust herself.

"Let's hope the other teams fare better than us," she said as they caught sight of Soteria once again, hovering over their gear and the unused probes.

"I'm buying the first round to drink to that," Trebec said. Then he stopped beneath the center of Soteria. Where they'd landed a few short hours ago.

Tasha and Langstad assumed their huddled positions with their commander. All clamped hands on one another's shoulders.

"Ready?" Trebec asked.

"Ready!" Tasha and Langstad both shouted.

"Engage homing beacon," Trebec said.

Then they squatted once again.

Tasha quirked up a half-smile, more than ready to return back to Earth. Eager to volunteer for another mission. Excited for the first time to take on whatever challenges came her way.

"See you on the flip side," she said.

IDYLLIC

THE WHOLE WORLD left a bad taste in Stephanie Gomez's mouth.

On top of the bitter coffee she'd gulped down not more than ten minutes ago in their ready room.

A bazillion scientists staring down at her crew didn't help.

Neither had becoming a part of the newly formed global Alt-Realm military.

Because the entire rest of the planet had gone bat-shit crazy.

After dedicating more than a decade of her life to the marines, she should have learned to go with the flow. That there were two worlds, military and civilian.

And she had. For a while.

Orders and authority. No problem.

Military structure? Good to go.

The mission to save humankind from an asteroid hurtling toward Earth?

Well... that had become debatable.

Because would identifying an alternate viable realm,

then transporting millions to that new world change anyone at their core? Wouldn't each person still have the same intelligence (or lack thereof), the same emotional state (unstable), and the same moral compass (questionable, at best).

Gotta save humanity from the inside out.

And that core had been rotting for centuries.

Still, she took a good hard look at the gawking White Coats, scanning around the recently completed world's largest stadium. Built of steel, concrete, and some top-secret rare earth elements. Complete with a bright strip of retracted skylights at the top.

Then she stared at the command platform. The wide glassed-in space housed the former top echelon of NASA. Plus Admiral Worthington, head honcho of Alt-Realm. And all of their respective underlings.

Why she gave each moment all she had.

For the cause.

Structure to the chaos.

Rules to be obeyed, without question.

For the greater good. For *humanity's* good.

No sides.

No selfishness.

Because we belong to everything... nothing belongs to us.

A phrase she'd heard from someone more enlightened than most. One she'd taken to heart.

Pumped to get their first mission underway, she bent her knees, bounced on her toes, and glanced at her fellow quantanauts.

They all wore clingy state-of-the-art environmental suits made of some nanotech material. With a full low-profile face visor, which displayed outer-environment readings in bright green in its smoky upper corners. Built-in tight but flexible gloves. Form-fitting nimble boots. Everything colored in the same quantanaut charcoal gray.

The suit purportedly sturdy enough to launch *rocketless* straight into another realm.

Everyone on their comm channel had gone radio silent in the last minutes before launch. Which made only the rasps of her own breaths filter into her ears.

And with every measured inhale, a sweet metallic scent laced the ionized air flowing into her helmet.

Ahead to her left, Commander Kate Salinger—only female commander among the five three-person quantanaut teams—stood a hair shorter than Stephanie, measuring five-nine, plus or minus. Born on American soil, to a half-First Nation mother and foreign-official British father, she'd gone straight into the marines like Stephanie had. Fresh out of high school. Eager to serve. Driven.

Both women leanly muscular.

Each with short hair.

But Commander Salinger had shorn her inky black strands close to her head. Making her sapphire-blue eyes pop against softly tanned skin.

Whereas Stephanie wore hers a bit longer, two inches all over, enough to give it a slight curl. Which she finger-combed through. Sometimes. And blackish brown eyes sank into the depths of her darker Latina complexion.

In contrast to them both and directly to her left, Doctor Sanjay Patel stood a diminutive five-six. With a small-boned frame. A soft-spoken voice. And pale gray eyes. But beneath his slighter stature and meek demeanor resided a brilliant mind and dedicated spirit. A valued member of their team.

All five of the quantanaut teams had been culturally and ethnically mixed by design. Prepared in case they encountered intelligent alien life at some point. Even though somehow their Team Four seemed to be the only crew who'd failed in obtaining a true-blooded white guy (or girl.)

Not that anyone could tell what any of them looked like. Not fully suited and helmeted.

With a vibrating *whomp*, their pre-jump probe popped into existence. The titanium instrument, the size of a basketball, plummeted to just above the ground, then hovered in place.

Materialized from a supernatural gateway that sprawled larger than life above them.

Named Soteria, after the goddess of salvation and deliverance. Because some cutesy amateur astronomer named the planet-killer asteroid Thanatos, Deliverer of Death.

Sure. Why not devolve us all the way back to the ancient Greek pantheon?

Feed the masses doom and gloom.

Bona fide golden tickets straight to Crazy Town.

Why Stephanie had distanced herself from all the hype.

And why she continued to pace herself with all the new, and unsettling, information.

But unable to hold back any longer, vibrating with rising anticipation, she finally tilted her head back and stared up into Soteria's mesmerizing depths. In person for the first time.

They'd been prepped for what to expect from the mechanism from their support team.

However, no amount of schooling conveyed the enormity of the real deal in action.

The massive gateway spanned an unbelievable three hundred meters long, and a good hundred fifty wide.

Up till that moment, she'd only seen the monstrosity in its inactive state. When the tubular figure-eight shape had been opaque dark-gray. And thanks to the secret-recipe mix of rare earth elements, hovering three meters above the concrete floor of the stadium. Center stage.

But today?

What a showstopper.

The outer membrane had gone wholly translucent.

Up within it, a dimensional field of velvety black sported a dusting of pinpoints of light. Multicolored and sparkling.

Not stars, or so they'd been taught in their five months of quantanauts training. Not in the traditional sense of gazing up into the night sky through a telescope.

No. Soteria somehow opened up a rift in the fabric of space and time. Where infinite alternate realms existed. Theorists debated over what actually lay on the other side of the portal. Alternate realities. Parallel dimensions. Wormhole shortcuts through space, to faraway planets.

Some argued all of the above. Claiming that the mechanics of it depended on perspective. And where the roulette wheel stopped.

Gathered from their collective experience after tens of thousands of probes had been tossed up into the thing by early scientists. At first, none returned. To this day, they have no idea where they'd all gone.

Then someone wised up and began outfitting the probes with the same rare earth elements as Soteria. They fashioned that connection into a kind of homing tag.

"Telemetry," Stephanie said into her helmet, beginning her role in the mission, anxious to get the show on the road.

Because their environmental suits pulled in atmospheric readings automatically, they knew the temperature in the jump zone had cooled considerably. Some subtle downdraft effect from Soteria, perhaps.

But they needed to get a bead on how things were on the flip side.

The hovering probe responded to her query by broadcasting pre-jump data from their destination world. Populating a stream of readings in bright green words and numbers on Team Four's visors.

Along with sending that data to the tablets of their two support specialists.

Their Earth-side scientist, Monica Wilson, monitored them from the ground-level perimeter, nine meters to their right. With her sleek long black hair, thick bangs, and watchful bright green eyes. Slender of frame, covered in perfect porcelain skin, she wore a crisp navy skirt-suit with a white collared shirt.

Team Four's jump facilitator, Tobias Carter, stood shoulder to shoulder with her. An older gentleman pushing eighty. Dark-skinned. Studious. He stared at their team over silver wire-framed eyeglasses, wearing his standard uniform: golf shirt (white today), weathered jeans, and bright orange running shoes.

Over the last two months, several dozen probes had gone to Team Four's specific destination. But in the last two days, six additional probes had been launched to verify that nothing had changed since discovery of the potentially viable realm. One probe on each of the two days at oh-six-hundred, at twelve-hundred, and at twenty-two-hundred hours.

Minutes ago, Monica and Tobias had tossed up the little pre-jump guy that just returned.

Behind them hovered three more probes, the ones that would be traveling with them for mission use. As well as a pale gray launch-and-land bundle, inflated protection around three gear cases and the weaponry strapped to them.

Farther ahead, a scattering of several golden containment fields covered some kind of litter on the jump floor. But no one on ground level seemed bugged about them. So Stephanie disregarded the oddity as irrelevant to the mission at hand.

Based on their pre-jump probe's telemetry, she determined the data matched all prior probe readings. Atmosphere. Humidity. Temperature. Pressure. And every other analog-type reading they'd been able to obtain. No imagery, not still photos nor video. No audio either.

Which had prompted the quantanaut teams to be assembled in the first place.

As explorers. Venturing bravely into the discovered new realms. Determining their viability firsthand. See and judge for themselves. Before sending millions of refugees through.

And their time had come.

"I'm *a go*." Stephanie gave a clipped nod.

"I'm *a go*," Patel concurred.

Monica and Tobias remained silent, per protocol. To keep their comm channel clear. The support team planned to intervene only if absolutely necessary. Because once they jumped way the hell out there? Team Four's crew were on their own.

They'd been heavily trained to prepare for any foreseeable circumstance. Cross trained in every discipline imaginable. Warfare and military strategy. Biology and medicine. Linguistics and culture. Archeology and art.

And focusing on all that charged brainpower, on honing her old skills and learning new, had helped balance her mind amid all the crazy.

The outer world had left such a bad taste in her mouth because the spectrum of mental cases—already on a knife's edge from societal drama and politics—had begun to fracture. With those in power self-destructively choosing to widen those cracks.

But Alt-Realm's mission to save their species made moral sense.

Worked toward a common goal.

Gave Stephanie hope for a better future. If not for the fracturing masses, at least for the innocents who still had time to grow into decent human beings.

"Tobias." Commander Salinger glanced at their jump facilitator. "I'm confirming *go* status."

"Go status, acknowledged," Tobias replied.

"On our countdown," Salinger said.

"Three." Stephanie widened her stance, gave a slight bounce once more.

"Two." Patel squared his shoulders.

"One," Salinger said. "And... *go.*"

Positioned in a wedge formation, with Patel to her left and Salinger ahead and between them, they did a deep squat as a team. Then in a bursting jump, they launched straight upward. As trained, they extended their arms as their momentum reached peak height.

And the moment their fingertips breached the last half meter near Soteria's membrane, the powerful energy from the gateway sucked them right in.

Stephanie stared wide-eyed into the vast inky blackness as she became one with it. For a split second, the multicolored pinpricks of light swirled.

Then searing pain lit every nerve ending on fire.

On instinct, she tried to gasp...

But found she couldn't breathe.

Couldn't see either.

No longer felt pain. No longer felt... anything

Somehow, she'd become everything. And nothing at all.

And then...

Absolute nothingness reigned supreme.

FROM THE ABSOLUTE NOTHINGNESS, a magnificent calming awareness blew up in Stephanie's consciousness.

Even while every other typical sense remained glaringly absent.

Like some giant sensory deprivation chamber had swallowed her whole.

Everything had vanished. That bitter coffee taste. The sweet metallic scent of ionized oxygen. Rasping sounds of her breaths. Tightness in her gloves and boots. The pinpricks of light and green readings from her visor. All gone.

In fact, she had no way to tell if she still breathed.

And yet, she only marveled at the bizarre effect. Unable to feel disconcerted about the loss of her faculties. Because an enormous sense of peace and rightness washed through her along with that heightened mental awareness.

What had she become?

Pure energy?

An elemental frequency?

No clue.

But not crazy. Not even chaotic. Nor stressed.

If she had to give a label to the sensation, she'd call it balanced. Nothing on the extreme. Right in the middle.

The amazing awareness enabled her to detect her two teammates, driven Commander Salinger and brilliant dedicated Patel. To know they were there, even without being able to communicate with them. Their supportive existence somehow seemed to press in, becoming a part of her. Even as her essence entwined with theirs.

Floating in the nothingness, time became irrelevant.

With no frame of reference, thoughts drifted in and out, like lazy clouds in an endless sky.

When the memory of a crazed humanity surfaced, it tempered into surrender, acceptance.

Then she wondered how all those unbalanced humans would fare through Soteria.

Would they find balance? Would they emerge fresh and new?

Would she?

Before she sensed any answer, an overwhelming tightness pressed in.

Alarm bells clanged into her ears. Accompanied by a too-calm AI voice warning that oxygen levels had fallen dangerously low.

Unimaginable pain returned, setting every nerve ending on fire.

So intense, in a last split-second thought, she thought they'd gotten tossed into a sun.

A HARD SMACKDOWN onto the ground corrected Stephanie's misunderstanding, ringing her bell. Hard.

Not thrown into a fiery sun.

Just catapulted through one.

Or maybe the molten lava of a volcano.

Some kind of major heat that scorched her ass.

Instead of bitter coffee, a coppery taste coated her tongue. Blood. After licking the tip around, she found a small wound where she'd bitten her lower lip.

A pungent scent filled her nostrils, in the few seconds sweet ionized air overcame the aroma. Likely from instant-response sweat. From the stress of volcano jumping.

After several deep breaths, the clanging warning bells ceased.

For the first time, she greatly appreciated the protective mechanisms of their dark-gray environmental suits. For not only providing life-giving oxygen, but also prompting its wearer to breathe.

And in those last fiery seconds, she'd thought maybe quantanauts were the craziest ones. For being the guinea-pig humans insane enough to jump through Soteria.

Not like the human race had a choice, though.

And somebody crazy enough had to blaze the trail.

So maybe everyone had gone a little nuts, her included.

Head still ringing from the hard impact, she blinked her eyes open.

A strange illumination glowed off something bright in front of her face.

"Tint off," she said. Commanding her smoky visor to shift full translucent.

A bluish light glowed in front of her face. Off a bright white surface.

Muscles sore, she pushed up off the ground. Then realized it wasn't the ground, as in somewhere outside, it was a floor... somewhere inside.

A bright white floor. With bright white walls about three meters apart. And a ceiling about three meters high. And an open doorway about a meter wide, with no door.

The bluish illumination seemed to come from the air itself.

She spun around, searching for the rest of her team.

And then she saw something... disturbing.

On the floor. In the far-left corner. A pair of dark-gray boots, toe-down. About the shoe size of Commander Salinger's. Attached to a portion of dark-gray environmental suited legs. And then white wall. Just below the knees.

"Commander?" Stephanie called out.

No response came through their comm channel.

"Commander Salinger!" she shouted more forcefully.

Nothing else existed in the stark space with her.

No Patel.

No Soteria hovering above, like they'd been trained would happen.

No probes.

No gear.

No weapons.

Nothing but Stephanie in a white room with one-third of Commander Salinger. Her stomach turned at the thought of what had happened to the other two-thirds.

Then she stared at the open doorway.

A quick second scan of the room confirmed no objects or furnishings of any kind existed in the room, only smooth white walls. Their finish a nonreflective suede, like the plaster of Greek seaside dwellings.

And the bluish illuminated air.

With measured steps, she crept toward the open doorway.

Through it, a hallway branched left and right, curving ever-so-slightly away in each direction. Slotted with similar open doorways evenly spaced apart, on both her side and opposite. No other life forms appeared.

And the bluish glowing air didn't seem disturbed by her movement. As if the blue substance didn't float in the air. More like the air itself emitted a blue phosphorescence.

She turned left and quickstepped through the hall

toward the nearest doorway. Hopefully toward an adjoining room. The other side of the disembodied boots-and-legs.

No movement or alarms sounded as she traveled through the hallway.

Slipping into the other room, unseen by whatever inhabitants had built the place, she spotted the remaining portion of Commander Salinger. Face-down. Unmoving.

The wall of the structure had a thicker depth than she'd imagined.

Because only another third stuck out into the adjoining room.

Commander Salinger's entire middle had materialized into the wall-space.

"Great," she muttered. One dead. And they hadn't even been there five minutes.

Or maybe just compromised?

"Kate Salinger!" she shouted, rushing toward her fallen teammate, thinking her given name might rouse the commander. "Get the hell up! No slacking on mission time!"

No response sounded.

"Gomez?" sounded a soft-spoken male voice.

"Patel!" She gusted out a sigh of relief. At least they were a team of two. "Where are you?"

"In the water." Breathy huffs sounded. "Swimming."

"Do you see Soteria?" she asked.

"Up above me," he said.

"The probes?" she asked. "Our gear?"

"Hovering and floating ahead of me." More huffing sounded. "I didn't want to deflate the gear." Another couple of huffs. "The inflatable's waterproof. For the moment."

"What do you see out there?" Somehow all those tossed

probes to their location must have either made it into one of the rooms or out where Patel was at.

But the larger transport of their team and gear had spread them out, over either side of the exterior of some building. And a wall.

She swallowed hard, staring down at the motionless Commander Salinger.

"Besides an ocean of water?" He paused to huff every few words. "A great walled city... Hundreds of tall skyscrapers... With metallic reflective sides... Massive thirty-meter seawall."

"Link one of those probes to me." She had an idea. And better to lead him somewhere safe.

"T4-513 to Gomez," he said.

"Track location," she directed the probe. "Guide. Patel to Gomez."

"ETA," purred the low female AI voice. "Ten minutes."

"Ah," Patel said. "The probe's angling toward a set of stairs in the seawall."

"Let me know if you need assistance," she said.

"We'll be okay." He huffed. "I'll have the probes... tow the gear inflatable."

"Watch for hostiles," she warned.

"Did you encounter any?" he asked.

"Negative." But better safe than sorry. "I'll scan now. We'll find out."

"Scan for lifeforms. Radius one kilometer," she directed her suit. Which would do two things. Assess Commander Salinger's condition. And alert them to any nearby inhabitants of the "great walled city" they'd dropped into.

"No lifeforms detected," the AI purred.

None. Not even her or Patel?

And no others. In a large city? With all those skyscrapers, each with multiple rooms?

"Identify Team Four quantanauts." Stephanie had a hunch on how to get the intuitive program to drill down its parameters.

"Sanjay Patel," the AI said.

"Vital signs of Sanjay Patel," she directed.

"Vital signs of Sanjay Patel," the AI said while populating his oxygen and pulse onto her visor.

"Vital signs of Stephanie Gomez," she said.

"Vital signs of Steph—"

"Cancel. Partition inquiry," she spoke over the AI. She knew her vital signs.

But partitioning her inquiry kept the next directive between her and the AI. So Patel wouldn't hear. He didn't need to worry. And they needed to focus on the mission.

"Vital signs of Commander Kate Salinger," she said.

"Vital signs of Commander Kate Salinger... Inconclusive," said the AI.

"Inconclusive?" She frowned. "Show Commander Kate Salinger's pulse and oxygen."

"No data available," replied the AI.

She sighed. Well, at least Salinger wasn't deceased. Or the AI would've said so. Maybe.

"Scan for lifeforms, no perimeter," she said. Without any idea of how far out their environmental suits could read. Unless, maybe the structure of the walls interfered with their suits' scanning abilities.

"No lifeforms detected," the AI repeated.

Out of curiosity, Stephanie reached out a glove to the white wall. Cognizant that the wall encapsulated a third of their commander.

When her fingertips touched the surface, it gave a little.

But not in a spongy way. The surface held firm and taut. But after the slightest resistance, her hand traveled *through* the wall.

But immediately, it fell ice cold. Then she lost all sensation in the hand.

She gasped and jerked her hand back out.

Pins and needles returned to her skin. Along with pinpricks of pain at every nerve ending.

With measured breaths, she rode out the pain as feeling slowly returned. That effect seemed like her hand had gotten frostbitten in an instant. Then began thaw.

The sounds of footsteps echoed down the hallway.

"That you, Patel?"

"And the probes," he said, appearing in the doorway seconds later after one probe, with two others following. "What?" He rushed into the room, but then stopped after a few strides, staring at Commander Salinger. "Is she..."

"Dead?" She gave a slight headshake. "Not according to our AI. Not alive either. And something's up with these walls. They're not totally solid."

"Weird blue light too." Sanjay stared at the empty room.

"What do you make of the place?" she asked. He'd traveled the farthest, seen the most.

"Feels weird. Like a ghost town. There are waterfalls in courtyards between buildings. Long mirror ponds and reflecting pools. Pathways made of this white material"—he pointed at the wall—"branching off toward multiple buildings. But no people."

"Or aliens," she pointed out.

"No alien life either," Patel agreed.

"AI says no lifeforms." She sighed. "I'm not buying it. Where did the builders of this city go?"

"It seems too well-kept to have been abandoned," he said.

"Maybe the bluish air keeps things tidy." She shrugged.

"We've got a problem, though," he said.

"Just one?" Aside from the fact their commander had been incapacitated? And their AI seemed unprepared to deal with the nature of the new realm.

"We can't access Soteria," he said.

She frowned. Then she stared up at the white ceiling. "It's above us, isn't it?"

"And out above part of that ocean, beyond that wall." He nodded above her shoulder. Past where Commander Salinger lay motionless. In some kind of stasis.

"But how did I... and the Commander... How did we come through the ceiling?" She stared at the white wall again. "The walls. And the ceiling. They're not *fully* solid. Maybe only partly in this world."

Patel moved toward the wall, reaching out with his glove.

"I wouldn't. Damn near froze my hand off inside that wall. Not sure if it's the wall itself or whatever lays between."

"Maybe we're not fully solid when we come out of Soteria," he said.

"Maybe..." But the problem remained. No way to jump back up into the last half meter of Soteria. Not if a ceiling barred the way. Even in its undefinable semi-solid state.

"Well, Commander Gomez..." He turned and saluted her. Indicating what she would've eventually realized. She'd become the one in charge by default. "What are our orders?"

"Map the place with two of the probes," she said. "Every wall, every ceiling."

"Under Soteria?" he asked.

"Under Soteria." She nodded. "Our goal is to find a viable world. We need to provide the safe zones to land in." Then she stared down at their fallen teammate. "Use Commander Salinger," she said, refusing to give up on her superior officer, "as a reference point. They'll have positioning of our original jump Earth-side. Hopefully that'll be enough of a ground zero to map the walls and grid out the jump zone on their end."

About all the sense they could make of the tricky landing area.

And they needed to ensure if millions came through, that they didn't get stuck inside weird freezing walls.

"Oh..." She suddenly realized a limitation. "Have the probes identify the floor above us, but while remaining *outside* of Soteria's perimeter. Don't have them go under—"

"Understood." Patel programmed the probes to map everything under the gateway, except for the last half meter above them, which would likely suck the probes back through to Earth prematurely.

Then he set both probes loose. They first scanned Salinger's location, the room they stood in, and then zoomed out, heading off in different directions.

Stephanie frowned, staring at the glow around them. "Let's also take a sample of this blue air."

Patel shook his head. "I left the gear at the seawall. All three probes and me could barely make it up the ladder. Didn't want to cause a delay, figuring out how to drag it all here."

"Right." She gave a nod. "Smart. Weapons?"

He shook his head. "Still inside. I didn't even want to risk deflating the thing. What if we need to go back into the water?"

"No." She stared over at their fallen teammate. "We can't go back that way. Not if we're all going back together."

FOR THE NEXT SEVEN HOURS, they investigated all they could of the abandoned city. While the two probes mapped the viable landing zones room by room. Twice.

The buildings stretched on and on, all bordered by a vast expanse of water that stretched toward the horizon.

They'd sent out the third probe to map an aerial of the place.

"Just... wow," she said. Still unable to believe what had risen up into the sky above the far side of the city.

"That *can't* be a planet." Patel gave a heavy blink at the thing.

"Maybe we landed on its moon," she said. They had only cross-trained in astronomy. Enough to recognize danger signs in a potential refuge. But not all realms gave up their secrets in their stars. Whatever the situation, both bodies in this realm rotated *really* close to one another.

Since their allotted time drew short, they made their way back to Commander Salinger.

"We're abandoning our gear?" he asked.

"No choice," she said as they returned. "Let's hope *we* are able to be recalled."

Since they weren't able to jump up into Soteria's capture zone, that last half meter, they'd have to rely on the nanotech homing chips in their environmental suits. Like the drones, those ingenious nanotech homing chips were their ticket back home in case they couldn't initiate a jump back on their own.

Stephanie hoped whatever quantum thing enabled

them to land *through* those bizarre walls, dematerialized all three of them enough to make it back through, going the other direction.

"Do you think it's vibration?" She stared up at the ceiling, wondering what made her and the commander come through it, but the commander get "stuck" in it.

Patel blinked. "Vibration," he repeated.

She tilted her head, confused. "Vibration?"

"Frequency. The wall," he said, staring at the bright white surface nearest him. "Solid, but not solid. Like it's here, but not."

"Not following..."

He glanced at her. "What if the city isn't abandoned at all? What if the lifeforms, the builders of this city are here right now? Just living in an alternate frequency?"

"Like actual ghosts?" She shivered. The idea creeped her out. Imagining other beings right with them, but on some alternate plane.

He snorted. "Just a crazy theory."

"So what's your verdict of this place?" she asked. "Viable?"

After a few seconds, he gave a nod. "Viable. Ghosts or not." He winked at her.

A large whomping vibration rippled through them.

Soteria activating.

The hovering probes swept up toward the ceiling then vanished.

"Come on, Commander Salinger," Patel said. "Hang in there."

"And whatever you are, weird walls and creepy abandoned place," she said. "Let us all go back unharmed."

Talking to the inanimate surroundings felt a little crazy.

And yet, after everything. It also felt right.

Seconds later, the world vanished.

Stephanie's whole body lit up in fiery pain.

And then absolute nothingness.

But not *total* nothingness.

Because once her consciousness blew wide again, and the peace and rightness and balance washed through her yet again, something else pressed in.

The solid awareness of her crew. Healthy and sound.

Her. Patel. *And* Commander Salinger.

Team Four? Mission success.

After having mapped out an idyllic realm.

Even if said realm might already be partially occupied.

But then...

Humans needed *something* in their new home to sensationalize.

JURASSIC

SHEER PANIC FLASHED through Lara Kim as she stood on the concrete floor of the jump zone. With the two permanent members of the quantanauts on Team Five.

This can't be happening.

The dark-gray environmental suit she'd put on for the first time an hour ago didn't help.

Thick state-of-the-art nanotech layers clung to her body, to every little nook and cranny. Built-in flexible gloves tightened around trembling fingers. Form-fitting boots hugged shifting feet. The thing's helmet cradled her skull like a swimming cap, arcing out only where an integrated visor curved over her face... two inches from her nose.

Claustrophobia anyone?

Breaths shallowing, pulse quickening, that arcing visor began to fog.

Which blocked out most everything else freaking her out.

Like the daunting stadium-effect of standing dead center in the world's largest concrete-and-steel hangar. With thousands of gawking white-coated scientists. And hundreds of NASA and Alt-Realm officials. Some monitoring the scientists along the concrete risers around the arena. Others assisting senior officers in a wide glass-walled command center that cantilevered above it all, midway toward her right.

Not to mention the unnerving astonishing phenomenon that hovered directly overhead. A massive quantum gateway. Powered up to fling Team Five into another world. Which she refused to look up at. Not yet. Not until she absolutely had to.

The gateway, named Soteria, had been created save the human race.

From the gigantic asteroid Thanatos, that hurtled toward Earth.

ETA? Six weeks.

In the blink of an eye, everyone's world would be turned upside down.

Or cease to exist.

And she balked at some job change?

Pull it together, Lara. No good options remained.

For what difference did it make in the grand scheme of things? Jumping now with a team of three... or in a mass evacuation of millions in few weeks?

Millions. Not billions.

Because the world had descended into chaos. And for logistics reasons alone, Alt-Realm knew it would be impossible to save them all.

After licking her lips, she forced a slow deep breath.

Saltiness laced the tip of her tongue.

A slight sourness tinged the air.

From breaking out in a nervous sweat.

Not from the clingy environmental suit; its technology supposedly purified her air.

No... the heaviest weight on her chest came from total unpreparedness.

She was never supposed to be one of the jumpers.

The contract she'd signed six months ago had said quantanaut team *support* scientist.

Yet she'd somehow gotten tapped to replace Team Five's field scientist.

Field scientist.

In an email mere hours ago. At the eleventh hour.

Of course, she'd fired off a curt refusal, balking at the ridiculous idea.

But she'd been overruled.

"Fine print of that very contract," her supervisor Barb had pointed out in another email. Backed up by an official legal order through email from her employer, Alt-Realm. The world's new military branch. "And Team Five demanded you be their third."

"But... what happened to their programmed third?" she'd emailed.

No reply came.

And when security showed up at her apartment door to escort her to the hangar, the reasons for the last-minute change got swept under the tide of other more pressing concerns. Amid a whirlwind crash course in everything she needed to know. In the hopes of surviving.

Because the rest of the quantanauts had all gotten five months of intensive cross-training to prepare—mentally and physically—to transport into another realm of existence.

She'd gotten a measly two-and-a-half hours.

Nowhere near enough time.

But plenty enough to freak out.

Black dots began to fringe her vision.

Tingles began to prick across her lips.

Closing her eyes, needing to find some kind of calm—so she didn't blackout on center stage—she drew in another deep breath of the oxygen mixture flowing in from her suit. The ionized air bore a metallic scent with a hint of sweetness. Like charged air before a thunderstorm.

While drawing in steadying breaths, she forced out panicky thought-fragments that spun through her mind. And as she focused all her attention on the sweet metallic air, with each next deep inhale and slower exhale, she began to feel marginally better. At least not in immediate danger of passing out.

She finally opened her eyes again.

The fog on her visor had begun to dry out. A feature of the suit's environmental systems.

Which is when she noticed the dark-gray helmeted form of another quantanaut striding toward them. Into the jump zone. Fully suited, helmet and all.

The newcomer came in from the perimeter on the far right. Where her colleagues, the other four team's lead scientists and jump facilitators had gathered. Outside of protocol.

Lara frowned. Total confusion replaced the panic.

Because each of the five jump teams only had three members.

She glanced ahead at the two permanent members of Team Five who'd drafted her. Commander Javier Rodriguez, a Mexican American from Arizona, stood tall and broad. Bo Duncan, born to a ranching family in South Dakota was a few inches shorter, but more muscular. Both men in their mid-forties had been career military, Navy for Javier, Army for Bo. Together the men operated as a well-oiled machine.

And they'd worked hard through their training over the

last five months. With an unwavering belief in Alt-Realm's cause. Highly intelligent, both had taken to Lara's rigorous instruction in the sciences well. Excelling in every discipline. Most especially biology, physics, chemistry, astronomy, and meteorology.

But something had obviously happened to their programmed field scientist, Helena Priam. The third perfect cog in their well-oiled machine. The one who'd cross-trained with both men for the entire five months. In each of the same disciplines. Beyond the sciences.

That woman had had the benefit of training with her team in everything from traditional warfare to guerrilla strategies. From running through zero-G obstacle courses to climbing mountains in simulated heavy gravity. In the harshest conditions, running the gamut from dry desert sandstorm to sweltering jungle swamp to freezing high-altitude blizzard.

Lara had only *trained them* in the physical *sciences*.

Not *trained with them*. Not getting *literally physical*.

Something she would've insisted upon, in hindsight.

Had she read the fine print.

Rodriguez and Duncan turned in unison toward the incoming person.

A third sent to relieve her?

Hope surged for the first time. That she wouldn't be subject to baptism by fire after all.

By the slight outline of breasts across the chest, Lara thought for a brief moment that the newcomer was Helena after all. Able to fulfill her programmed role.

But an instant later, she realized the woman had a slimmer build and stood a hair taller than Helena, a good half foot taller than Lara's petite five-one.

The newcomer's visor reflected bright sunlight

streaming down from the hangar's retracted skylights, making it impossible to see a face behind it. Until the woman stepped into the shadow of Soteria, when the visor became partially transparent. But with the few meters still between them, Lara only made out partial features, dark arches of brows, dark irises within the whites of her eyes.

"For the record, I think this is a really bad idea," said a low female voice.

"Clarissa?"

Lara recognized their other support specialist, Clarissa James. Team Five's jump facilitator. The person tasked with training their crew of three on what to expect going through the gateway, as best anyone could. How to approach initial entry. What to do to minimize travel pains. And theories on best landing practices. Theories on all of it, really. Because no one knew for sure. Nothing seemed to be constant. And probe telemetry had been limited.

"In the flesh." A heavy sigh sounded. Then Clarissa turned toward the guys. "Against my *strenuous* objections, Commander."

Rodriguez dipped his helmet a fraction. "Noted."

"Why are *we* here, again?" Lara asked. As if they'd been told the reason once before. None of it made sense. All five quantanaut teams were comprised of three people. All of mixed nationalities and cultures, by design of Alt-Realm's first-contact protocol. At least one man and one woman. But never two of each.

"Because Team Five needs *both* of you," Commander Rodriguez replied.

"But what happened to—" A whomping vibration caught her off guard.

Team Five's titanium pre-jump probe dropped into existence, just ahead of their position, from three meters up.

Out of the depths of Soteria. The device plummeted toward the concrete jump pad, then stopped and hovered just above the ground.

"Telemetry," Duncan said, staring at the probe.

The probe replied, providing them readings of their destination world in a stream of green numbers and words at the top corners of each of their visors.

Right. So they weren't going to discuss why she and Clarissa had been drafted.

"Guess we're the token sacrificial females," Lara muttered.

Commander Rodriguez turned, then strode over. He squared off with her, shooting her an unyielding stare, clearly visible at the close range through their visors. "You are a valuable member of our team." He turned toward Clarissa. "Both of you. And we need you to focus on the mission. Concentrate on what we need to do now. Not why any of us are here or where we'd rather be."

"All clear," Duncan replied. "I'm *a go.*"

"Are you with us?" Commander Rodriguez asked, staring at Clarissa.

Clarissa hesitated, then gave him a nod. "I'm with you."

"I'm with you," Lara replied, refusing to allow her panic to surface again.

Because in the end, the whole world counted on Alt-Realm and its exploring quantanaut teams. And like it or not, she'd become a needed field operative for Team Five.

"And you've reviewed the telemetry?" the commander asked.

Something they all were expected to do, throughout their mission.

Lara scanned over the readings once more, assessing the

conditions of the environment they were about to jump into.

"Yes," Clarissa replied. "All readings match. I'm *a go*."

"I concur," Lara said.

A heavy sense of calmness washed through her. Staying out of her head, immersing herself in data, and following orders kept the fear at bay. *One step at a time.* A mantra Clarissa had instilled through the last crash-course hours. One Lara planned to rely on.

And the probe's readings were solid. Matched the readings from the three probes sent the day before, within acceptable tolerances. And matched the three probes from the day before that. Their destination landing zone remained stable.

Of course, they didn't know much more about their destination realm than the basic analog readings the probe provided. Only that the environment seemed a viable option to sustain human life.

Commander Rodriguez swiveled his head toward Lara. The dark slashes of his brows raised, as if expecting something further.

"Oh...yes..." Lara swallowed hard. "I'm *a go*."

Alt-Realm's green-light terminology, per protocol. Each member of the team had to verbally agree that the mission would proceed. And they were required to do so independently. Any reservations? And the team paused, assessing further.

Lara had a mountain of reservations. But every last one of them were her own personal demons. An innate desire to remain behind the scenes, immersed in data, distanced from physical action of any kind. And far removed from having to deal with too many people. Or be part a group dynamic. But not one of those were mission viability related.

In the last seconds of her feet being planted firmly on planet Earth, she finally gazed up into the depths of Soteria.

"Whoa," Lara murmured, transfixed by an enormous dark and unimaginable beauty.

She'd only ever seen Soteria in its inert state. An opaque dark-gray. Three hundred meters long and half that wide. Fashioned into an infinity shape. Made with some combination of rare earth elements and the brilliant minds of inventive quantum pioneers.

But for their jump, the whole mechanism had shifted translucent to reveal something... *mind-blowing*.

Forcing deep breaths—trying not to freak out so she didn't set off her environmental suit's alarms—she stared into the gateway, created to transport humankind into other realms.

Inky blackness yawned above them, like a bottomless canyon ripped into the fabric of space and time. Within its darkness, pinpricks of colored lights sparkled. And as she stared at one fixed point, the multicolored pinpricks and inky blackness took on a layered dimension, moving in a near-imperceptible swirl.

A bump jarred her from her awestruck state, and she glanced right.

Clarissa nudged shoulders with her. "Nuthin' to it. Remember the steps I walked you through in the ready room."

Lara swallowed hard, then nodded. "Deep breath, deep squat, punch up with full-body power, arms up at maximum height."

Clarissa, the team's jump facilitator, gave her a nod. "Perfect. And we'll do it together. Side by side."

"Admiral Worthington," Commander Rodriguez said. "We're *a go*."

"Go status confirmed," Admiral Worthington replied.

"On our count," the commander said, then gave a nod toward Duncan.

"Three," Duncan said.

When Clarissa her a nod of encouragement, Lara said, "Two."

Clarissa waited a half second, then said, "One."

"And... *go!*" Commander Rodriguez said.

After a deep breath, Team Five flowed as one unit in their loose square formation. Rodriguez and Duncan side by side in front. Lara and Clarissa a meter behind them. They deep squatted, then burst up, extending their arms up in unison to reach that last half meter of charged space below Soteria's invisible lower membrane.

Through the fingertips of her gloves, Lara felt the power of the gateway engage. Then a strange electrical tingling rippled through her like wildfire.

And in that split second of contact, mysterious Soteria sucked her into another dimension.

THAT INITIAL CHARGED TINGLING FLARED into an unbelievable pain, Lara's whole body lighting up as if every single nerve ending had been set aflame.

And then, another split second later... nothing.

The pain vanished.

In fact, all sensation did.

Cast into some enormous void, she no longer felt any connection to her physical body. No salty taste from her lips. None of the sweet metallic scent of her helmet's oxygen. Nor the tightness from her environmental suit. Or the soft rasping of her shallowed breaths. No inky blackness stretching forth, no pinpricks of multicolored lights.

No sensation. Whatsoever.

But in the instant it took to realize all that, her mental awareness... exploded.

As if she'd been transformed into pure consciousness. And nothing else.

And when thoughts of her three teammates popped into her mind, awareness of their spiritual essence pressed in too. She couldn't speak with no mouth, nor hear without ears, yet she felt them there with her, all the same. As some sort of vibration. Maybe.

An enormous sense of peace washed through her. Acceptance of the present moment. Without need of the how or the why of it all.

Memories intact—sharpened even—random thoughts floated in and out of her mind, like image-filled drifting soap bubbles.

And for the first time that day, since that alarming email of her being assigned as a field scientist on Team Five's jump, she thought of her fiancé, Bryan.

Well, *ex*-fiancé.

Over a week ago, they'd gotten into a massive fight. And parted ways because of it.

As a firefighter, he'd been dealing daily with the psychological fallout of the world coming to an end. Dealing with the heartbreaking mess of those who'd ended their lives before the asteroid had any chance to. And fevered attempts at saving those they could: people on the edge of rooftops preparing to jump, botched drug overdoses, crazed gun-wielding citizens. Not to mention treating the escalating physical injuries. From chaotic riots of hundreds and thousands all the way down to two arguing neighbors who'd devolved to punches over deferred yard care.

Bryan wanted to get married immediately. And work on getting pregnant yesterday.

Lara thought he'd gone off the deep end too.

Earth had six weeks left.

If they were able to find a viable realm to escape into, and that was still a big *if*, whyever would they risk bringing a child into a brand-new world they knew nothing about?

And that was assuming they were among the lucky few chosen to emigrate there.

All the rest, multiple billions, would perish in an instant on the impact.

Or suffer a horrific death, if scientists somehow got their estimates wrong.

"All the more reason to get pregnant, Lara!" Anger had riddled his tone in their first-ever emotionally charged fight over their eight-month relationship. "We're young and strong. I'm a first responder. You're a scientist. Don't you think we'd be the first to go?"

"But go *where*?" she'd argued, voice barely above a whisper. "What kind of world is it? Even if the new realm has a perfect climate, what about unknown viruses and bacterium? What about the predator/prey situation? What about weather phenomenon and seasons? Or other threats we know nothing about?"

With a slow headshake, she said, "No. I won't bring a child into that unknown world. Not for a while. Not until we know the risks."

He'd taken two steps backward at her reasoning, like she'd shoved him with her words. He crossed his arms. "In that case, don't you want to live for the now?" Hurt and betrayal flashed across his face. As if she'd cast him adrift. As if he no longer believed in the deep love she felt for him.

"I am." She'd sighed heavily, just as gutted by the sudden divide between them as he. "I'm living for the hope of our species. Putting all my efforts and belief into the success of Soteria. Hoping some of us get to go."

"Even if that 'some of us' isn't... *us?*"

That last weighted word had hung there, deadly in the great divide yawning between them.

"Even if." She'd swallowed hard, tears welling in her eyes.

"Then we're done." He'd spun on his heel, packed a duffle full of clothes, then stormed out of their apartment.

Eight days prior.

No emotional scars from that fight filtered into the vast nothingness of Soteria.

Only the memory.

But, in the absence of emotion, she wondered at Bryan's belief. Then at the beliefs of the human race in general.

Wouldn't everyone be taking a risk?

Even if Alt-Realm managed to get ten million through before disaster struck—which over forty days, meant ten thousand people an hour through the only gateway they had, round the clock—almost nine billion more would perish on Earth.

And the lucky ones who made the jump through Soteria, to safety, they'd be pioneers. Colonists of an entirely different realm.

Inherent in that benefit were the risks that came with it.

So if Alt-Realm succeeded in their high hope of transporting through ten million, the survivors would be on their own. To fend for themselves. Through trial and error, sickness and healthy, life and death, they'd need to adapt. Or all their efforts would have been for naught.

Which made Lara wonder if Bryan had expressed a valid point.

And she'd been too narrow-minded to see the bigger picture.

No emotion accompanied that nugget of personal growth.

Only the cold hard realization.

An instant after that awareness, excruciating pain set every nerve ending ablaze. Again.

And then, sensation returned.

Awareness of her entire body.

Bright light activated the smoky tint of her visor.

Deafening warning bells clanged into her ears.

She gasped for oxygen.

All while she plummeted headfirst into another realm.

SOLID SHINY BROWNNESS raced toward Lara's face.

Red lights blinked across her smoky visor.

Above the clanging warning bells, a low female AI voice warned, "Low oxygen." Immediately followed by, "Impact imminent."

The sweet metallic air provided by her environmental suit filled her lungs.

Saltiness laced the tip of her tongue as she pulled her lips in.

All while she tucked her chin to her chest, throwing her weight forward, doing her best to curl into a rotating ball.

She crashed landed, the bottom of her neck and shoulders taking the brunt of the impact. But instead of rolling.

She unrolled. Center back. Hips. Legs. Boots. Then stuck fast and hard.

And instead of the flaming all-consuming pain to every nerve ending through Soteria, she barely felt the impact. Like she'd accidentally tumbled onto thick carpet.

When she tried to lift her limbs, resistance held them down.

"Uh... guys?" Lara stared up at the dark shadow of Soteria, rimmed by a bright grayish-white sky.

Silence followed.

Then a couple of low grunts sounded through her helmet's comm.

"Everyone okay?" she tried again.

"Team Five, roll call," Commander Rodriguez ordered in his authoritative bass voice. "Report condition."

"Lara Kim," she said, unsure if he expected full names. But then, when hit hard in the head, rescue personnel always asked the victim for the year and if they knew who the president was. "Unharmed. But unable to move. I'm... stuck. To the ground." Whatever ground in the new realm meant.

"Bo Duncan," sounded a second deep voice. "Five by five. We landed in swampy marsh. I've got your six, Kim. En route now, Commander."

"Fives and sixes," Lara muttered. "English, please. Remember us girls didn't train with you military boys."

"Five by five means I'm good," Duncan said as her clanging bells finally cycled off. "Got your six, means I've got your back."

A shadow blocked the overhead brightness.

Slight weight pressed outside each of her thighs.

Strong hands gripped each of hers and gave a yank upward, then forward.

101

"James?" Commander Rodriguez asked.

No reply came.

Lara scanned the terrain of what surface they'd landed in. It looked giant mud bog. Shiny wet brownness stretched toward the horizon. Like a giant evaporated lake bed. Some distance away, in multiple directions, dark smudges resembling low-handing clouds hovered over the mud.

Not far from their location, a large round pale gray inflatable sat atop the mud, which she knew held three gear cases along with their weaponry strapped to it. Protected by its outer cushioning in the event of a hard or difficult landing. Three titanium mission drones hovered beside the inflatable.

She unstuck her boots one at a time from the muck, then turned around.

In the opposite direction from the gear inflatable and drones, about fifty meters back, plant life exploded. Lots of green. Tall trees that stretched hundreds of meters high, blotting out the sky above it. Thick rainforest. Or jungle, maybe.

"Locate Clarissa James," Commander Rodriguez ordered their AI companion.

"Clarissa James located," the low female AI voice purred an instant later.

"Map directions to Clarissa James."

A terrain map populated their visors.

A trio of solid green dots marked each of their locations. Her and Duncan together. The commander a couple of meters ahead. A fourth red dot blinked. In between. But much fainter.

"Duncan?" Confusion marked the commander's tone. "Did you walk straight to Kim?"

"Yes, sir." Bo turned around. "Didn't spot James at all."

Directly above them, Soteria hovered. The gateway stretched long and wide in their new realm, just as it did on Earth-side. Same inky blackness in its depths. Same multicolored pinpricks of light.

Relief coursed through her at the familiarity of Soteria. Even though, just moments ago Earth-side, sheer panic at transporting through it the first time had immobilized her.

She'd survived the jump.

And felt immense gratitude at knowing the gateway remained open on the destination side.

To be able to transport them back.

Yet with a deep frown, she stared back down at the stretch of mud where Cassandra's faint red dot blinked. "Could she be under the mud?"

All three of them triangulated toward the red dot. Till the trio stood on top of it, according to their visor maps.

"Cassandra?" she called out. Just to be sure she hadn't missed anything, she stared up. But only the inky blackness stretching up there. Along with those multicolored pinpricks.

Duncan squatted down. Then he tightened his fingers together, forming a spear with his hand and upper arm.

Directly above the location of the faint red dot, Duncan pressed downward. When his elbow hit mud, he leaned into it. When his shoulder hit the surface, he said, "Commander? Grab my gear belt?"

An instant later, Commander Rodriguez slipped his gloved fingers into the dark-gray webbing of Duncan's belt.

Once anchored, Duncan pressed down farther, until his helmet disappeared. Soon his other shoulder vanished along with half his chest.

Nervousness spiked through her. How far did the mud bog extend? Had Clarissa sunk to its depths?

A muffled low noise sounded. Duncan? Whatever he'd said registered as indiscernible tones. Vibrations, really.

Then Duncan kicked a leg out, nailing the commander in the shin.

"Got it," Commander Rodriguez grumbled. "Pull you up."

When the commander struggled, Lara rushed over and hooked her gloved fingers into his webbing belt. And the both of them, in a makeshift tug-of-war chain, slowly began moving backward.

Little by little, Duncan's body reappeared, coated in thick mud. Shoulders. Neck. Helmet. Elbow. Hand.

Then a foot, attached to his hand. Soon a leg. A hip. Another bent leg. Torso. Arms. Then a second helmet. All completely coated.

"—ly shit!" Clarissa shouted. "Thought I was a goner, for sure. Couldn't move a damn muscle. Couldn't hear a thing besides my own screaming."

Lara rushed over and scraped muck off her teammate's visor.

"Thanks." Clarissa gave her a weak smile through the smeared lens.

Clarissa stared down at the clean front of Lara's environmental suit. Then she glanced at the commander's cleanish suit. Before staring around at the massive muddy lake bed. "How the hell did you guys not get sucked down?"

Duncan scraped mud off his own visor. "James, you must've swan dived straight down. The rest of us did some form of a roll."

Clarissa sighed heavily, then stared up at Soteria. "Well, scratch this place, then. No way we'll transport thousands at a time without losing most of our refugees."

Because they couldn't move Soteria. They had no way

to control where the gateway appeared. And based on repeated probe readings, scientists had determined with relative certainty that the gateway opened in each world in the exact same location. Without fail.

"Let's not call it a mission failure," Commander Rodriguez said. "Alt-Realm might figure out a way to catch everyone. Maybe. We aren't here to figure out landing logistics. That's their job. We're here to assess realm viability. Nothing more."

Duncan gave a nod. "I'll assign the probes to scan the area."

"I'd like to check out those smudgy cloud things," Lara pointed toward the several hovering masses beyond the gear inflatable."

"James, go with Kim." Commander Rodriguez stared out toward the larger green mass of trees. "Duncan, you assign the probes. Then you're with me into the jungle. Switch to channel two comms."

"Ten four, Commander."

"More numbers," Lara muttered.

"Eh," Clarissa said as they tromped as lightly as possible, trying not to sink with each step. "If it keeps them in their comfort zone, let 'em speak numbers all day long."

With the careful trudging through the mud, it took them a good five minutes before they got within a hundred meters of the smudges.

"What *are* those things?" Clarissa asked, stopping to stare.

"I..." Lara blinked, pausing with her. "...have no idea."

The hovering masses of plant life defied the known laws of Earth physics. But then again, less than a year ago, so had Soteria.

The size of a two-story house, a mushroomy drab brown

dirigible floating above. And underneath, plant life hung down in every hue of green imaginable. Pops of purples and pinks and yellows and blues seemed to be different shaped flowers. Small hovering things bounced from color to color.

"Zoom image," Lara said. "The top seems different than the bottom."

"Share zoomed image," Clarissa said. "Looks like a giant dried cap of... soil?"

"That's exactly what it looks like," Lara said. She turned to face the other smudges. "They're like upside-down islands of life. Over the mudflat."

"Calculate humidity," Lara said.

"Eighty-four percent humidity," purred the AI.

"Hmmm..." Lara stared at the dirigible's dry cap on top. "Something must be in the mud to prevent the plants from growing in it."

"Acidic, maybe," Clarissa said. "Or maybe nothing but mud all the way down. No life in the soil."

"But life in the air." Definitely insects or animal pollinators, judging by the bouncing hovering things. "Microbes. Moisture. Maybe some of the mud in infinitesimal particles formed the caps on top."

"Protecting it from..." Clarissa spun in a circle, staring up at the bright grayish-white sky. "Ummm... is there a sun in this realm? What's all the white stuff?"

"Maybe a different kind of cloud cover than we're used to. Or a layer of atmosphere different from one of Earth's?" All things the scientists who migrate to the muddy place would have the rest of their lives to ponder and test.

"Back to the jump zone!" Commander Rodriguez shouted. "Now!"

Heavy breaths sounded over their comms. "Got about twenty seconds before we're outflanked."

Lara frowned as she turned with Clarissa. Then the two girls began a slow-trudge back. "Outflanked?"

"Yep!" Duncan said. "Big sons-of-bitches, too."

"Does it sound like the guys are running?" Lara asked.

"It does." Clarissa glanced at her through her mud-smeared visor. "Not like we can do anything about it. The harder we punch down with our legs, the deeper we sink in the mud."

"Telemetry!" Duncan shouted.

Data streamed down their visors. Images of enormous beasts. With teeth.

Clarissa let out a slow breath. "I thought the probes couldn't capture any images."

"Apparently they can." In color. And threatening detail. "Maybe Soteria wipes all the data." All but the analog readings they'd been able to glean.

A deafening roar reverberated into their ears.

"Somebody's pissed," Commander Rodriguez said.

Clarissa and Lara managed to quick-trudge with light fast steps halfway back to Soteria by the time Rodriguez and Duncan broke out of the jungle.

"Split up," Commander Rodriguez said.

Duncan veered right, the commander left.

And they appeared to quick-trudge the best they could, distancing themselves from one another and from the jungle.

Two seconds later, four massive creatures exploded out of the jungle. Each had fuzzy long green bodies atop countless skinny stilt-like legs. Gaping mouths at the front of those long bodies had rows of white daggers for teeth.

"Uh..." Clarissa stopped dead in her tracks. "What's with the giant shark-toothed giraffe-legged caterpillars?"

"Wonder what the butterflies look like..." Lara muttered.

Yet the moment those stilt-like legs hit the mud, the creatures faltered, legs stuck down hard and fast. And with their forward momentum, the scary dagger teeth of their long green bodies face-planted straight down into the mud.

The men kept on trudging forward.

Lara and Clarissa resumed their quick-trudge, angling toward Soteria's shadow.

A couple minutes later, the foursome all met together, huffing from the exertion.

"Right. So we're not gonna stick around," Duncan said.

"We're not?" They hadn't even undone their gear. She'd hoped to obtain samples. Examine the plant life.

"No." Commander Rodriguez gave a hard headshake.

"Definitely no." Duncan stared back toward the jungle. "Those things were the *smallest* wildass things we saw."

"And the other creatures fly." The commander stared toward the jungle.

"Butterflies?" Clarissa snorted.

"Sure." Commander Rodriguez glanced at Clarissa. "If butterflies are the size of commercial airliners. And suck the life out of elephants the size of cement trucks."

"Yeah, I'm good," Clarissa said, standing under Soteria.

"But... did we have mission success?" Lara asked.

"Maybe. The *world* is viable." Commander Rodriguez sighed. "But this primitive cesspool is like Jurassic Park all over again. Alt-Realm will have a devil of a time figuring out how to protect humans in this predatory world."

Duncan recalled the probes.

Commander Rodriguez left the gear and weaponry in the inflatable. Sitting there atop the mud.

Once they gathered in a square formation again, a strange buzzing echoed into their comms.

"Skip the countdown!" Commander Rodriguez snapped his face toward the jungle.

"One!" Duncan shouted, right as the commercial-airliner butterflies arrowed out from the mass of greenery.

"And *go!*" Commander Rodriguez said as they squatted down, then burst upward.

Lara tore her gaze from the giant carnivorous insects and stared up into the depths of Soteria as she extended her arms.

Tingling flashed across her fingers right as she thought of Bryan.

And in that split second, she knew.

Once she returned to Earth, she planned to hunt down Bryan.

And they would live in the moment.

Because if the man she loved wanted to make a baby with her on the cusp of the end of the world?

Then they would sort things between them.

And have sex like bunnies.

All while Alt-Realm figured out how to save them all.

Or at least the lucky few...

Thank You!

Thank you for adventuring off Earth with us in *Braving Soteria: A Quantanauts Collection*.

If you enjoyed the stories, please express your love for *Braving Soteria: A Quantanauts Collection* by recommending it to friends in person, by email, on Goodreads, and through book clubs and reader groups.

And if you value reviews to help guide you into your next book, as we do, please help other readers by sharing your review of *Braving Soteria: A Quantanauts Collection* on your favorite retailer and book community sites.

Incredible thanks to everyone for extending your love of *Braving Soteria: A Quantanauts Collection*.

Reviews are cherished love notes to authors
and tantalizing invitations to readers.
Appreciated by all. ♥

Want to Read More?

Escape into award-winning time travel romance in the novels of the **Highland Legends** series...
Forged in Dreams and Magick
Bound by Wish and Mistletoe
Born of Mist and Legend
Found in Flame and Moonlight

Adventure in a paranormal short-story series, a spinoff of the Highland Legends series
THE TRAVELER: Initiate Years ...
Veil of Realms
Secrets of Alexandria
Panther Rising
Stones of Power
Highland Magick

Dive into the romance of the
No Weddings series...
No Weddings
One Funeral
Two Bar Mitzvahs
Three Christmases
For Valentine's

The first four novels can be found in...
No Weddings Limited Edition Box Set: Books 1-4

Read more of your favorite characters from the No Weddings series in the spinoff
Unbreakable Series...

Kiki & Darren's romance ignites in...
Heartbreaker

Mase & Leilani's passion flares in...
Rule Breaker

Ben & Shay flirt with danger in...
Lawbreaker

Want to Read EVEN More?

Quantanauts Genesis
Icebreaker and ***Ball Breaker***
are all coming soon!

Be the first to receive preorder alerts, exclusive bonus gifts, and occasional free stories...

Join our Bastion Family Adventurers!
https://www.katbastion.com/email-subscription/

ALSO BY KAT & STONE BASTION

THE TRAVELER: Initiate Years

Veil of Realms · Secrets of Alexandria · Panther Rising
Stones of Power · Highland Magick

Highland Legends Series

Forged in Dreams and Magick · Bound by Wish and Mistletoe
Born of Mist and Legend · Found in Flame and Moonlight

Unbreakable Series

Heartbreaker · Rule Breaker · Lawbreaker
Forthcoming: *Ball Breaker · Icebreaker*

No Weddings Series

No Weddings · One Funeral
Two Bar Mitzvahs · Three Christmases
For Valentine's

Standalone Novels & Novelettes

Brand New Year · The Espionage Effect

Romantic Poetry for Charity

Utterly Loved

Quantanauts Genesis

The hovering four-man escort—in crisp Air Force dress blues with flight caps perched on their heads—bordered on civilian harassment for one lone guy.

No matter how many regulations Rafe Medina had bent over the years.

Or how many federal laws had been broken.

...in the last few months.

None of which he'd been caught in the act of.

No cameras.

No trails.

No witnesses.

And a good couple of weeks had passed since his last transgression. A minor trespass. Not one thing stolen. Nothing even borrowed. That time.

Even so, the blue penguin stiffs had shown up at his single-room mountain cabin that rainy Sunday morning. With orders requesting his presence—from the Joint Chiefs of Staff.

He'd stood there in the doorway barefoot. In a rumpled black T-shirt and gray sweats. Favorite white diner coffee mug in his left hand. Official-looking order in his right.

Speechless.

And mildly amused.

But the buzzing curiosity about whatever the big boys at the Pentagon could want with a mid-thirties adrenaline junky won him over.

117

He'd made his escorts wait outside. A good thirty minutes.

They'd chosen to stand in the steady drizzle—instead of the stately comfort of their glossy black helicopter, parked in a grassy meadow eighty yards back, alongside the muddy dirt-road track leading in. Two had taken quasi-shelter under a dripping hundred-foot western white pine, at ease, but facing the cabin's front door and its two flanking windows. The third and fourth had stood guard a few yards off each front corner, sweeping vigilant gazes down the length of his freshly chinked log walls.

Watching for what? A desperate escape?

That would require fear. Or some semblance of guilt. Maybe even a dislike for politics. Or the long reach of the federal government.

None of which he held in any abundance.

No, his meter for all things governmental ran closer to apathy, in general. Mixed with a strong aversion to authority, when directed toward him specifically.

However, the Pentagon summons had been phrased *We humbly request your presence at a briefing of the utmost urgency...* Humbly. Request. Like a weird party invitation. Tagged with a healthy attempt toward guilt at the end. As if the world might end, so better not let it down.

Which had made the unexpected red-carpet treatment —toward an insignificant extreme-sports enthusiast—more of an intriguing turn of events. Something to investigate, not avoid.

So while the blue penguin squad had kept a watchful eye on the wet exterior of his cabin, he'd finished his juicy two-pound ribeye breakfast.

Then he'd changed into *his* standard uniform: lightweight thermal top, durable tactical pants, pair of zero-drop hiking boots. All in black. The best color: all in one.

Fast-forward to the here and now, and the decorators at the Pentagon apparently agreed: the darker, the better.

Because five pairs of boots echoed down a corridor that stretched on forever, deep in the bowels of the federal military fortress. Its floor, walls, and ceiling, all swathed in shiny black.

Without breaking his laidback stride, Rafe took another pull of hot coffee, with a single firm tap of his left forefinger on the white to-go cup. Force of habit. Small idiosyncrasy from childhood. Quirky, according to women who'd passed through his life. Control mixed with a reality check, at the heart of it.

And he'd insisted on the refueling pitstop, tasked the penguin stiffs to search out the highest-rated coffeehouse in D.C.

Because they'd "escorted" him across the country all damn day. From Northern Idaho.

He'd tolerated a fifty-five-minute helicopter ride, a four-hour flight from one Air Force base to another, then an eternal crawl through evening rush hour at the tail end. All silent, save for cursory *yes's* or *no's* and plenty of *I'm not at liberty to say's*. His hearty ribeye breakfast still stuck rock solid with him, but that original coffee needed a boost.

The quad-shot Americano he'd picked up, from some hole-in-the-wall the locals swore by, wasn't half bad. Had a rich nutty flavor with a touch of bitterness. Which matched him well.

The echoing black corridor ended at a set of steel double doors.

His lead penguin rapped three times against the door on the right.

Two seconds later, a heavy thunk sounded and the door cracked open.

A bald brown head popped out, attached to broad shoulders covered in an unrecognizable dark-gray uniform with black epaulets. The guy swept a glance across the penguin squad, landed a calculating gaze on Rafe, then pushed the door halfway open.

"Been nice knowin' ya, boys." Rafe lifted his coffee in salute to the tight-lipped stiffs.

Then he strode forward, ready to get to the bottom of the bizarre summons.

A situation room larger than ten of his cabins spanned forward and wide, buzzing with dozens of low conversations. Standing room only along the perimeter. All the uniformed branches represented in their dress whites, greens, and blues. Plus the latest blackish-blue of Space Force. And more than a few in that same unfamiliar gray as the door guard, so dark it edged toward black.

Down the center of the room stretched a mahogany conference table, seating twenty to either side and four to an end.

Some dark gray metal sheathed the back and side walls, floor to ceiling.

Black rubber flooring spanned underfoot.

A hodgepodge of scents hovered thick in the packed expansive space. Reminded him of a carnival. Notes of caramelized burnt mixed with cloyingly sweet, from coffee and pastries on a sideboard hugging the right wall. Accompanied by a hint of something metallic, like machine oil. And the sour tang of old sweat, not quite masked by fading deodorant residues and clashing perfumes and colognes.

Rafe never wore any of that crap.

Commercialism had brainwashed the American public

into believing they stank. Clean bodies fed by balanced diets didn't stink. But a few overweight malnourished diabetics, in old cakey deodorant, made a room full of stressed corporates reek like a ripening garbage dumpster.

In a valiant attempt to reboot his senses, he took a longer pull of his Americano and rolled the strong brew over his tongue before swallowing.

Twelve muted monitors—covering the width of the far wall, three rows down and four across—displayed various images. Some played news or graphic videos. Others featured still images, resembling NASA telescope photographs.

NASA.

Rafe scanned the room again. Aside from all the military uniforms, over a dozen men and women garnered a more important seat at the table, sporting casual longer hairstyles and business dress. Men in jackets, shirts, and ties. Women in sharp suits.

Lower-classed military, from every faction, were the ones hugging the perimeter.

Maybe six military officers sat at the table, aside from the Joint Chiefs.

Only one seat remained open.

Midway down the table.

Beside a woman, late-twenties...thirty tops, who stared at him with open curiosity.

She had shiny brunette hair with a slight wave to it, shoulder length. Light-brown complexion. Roundish face. Pale soft eyes. Gray maybe? Slender arching brows. Full lips. Pretty, in an understated way.

But then, those pale soft eyes hardened, narrowing at him.

Don't like my outfit, sweetheart?

Wouldn't be the first time he'd been judged on appearance.

Then again, he'd never subscribed to being told what to wear. Why he'd never gone military. Or corporate. Those issues with authority.

The scrutinizing beauty wore casual clothing. More business-casual than sport-casual (like him), but different than all the other stiff suits and uniforms.

On a hunch the empty seat had been left open for him, he cut left, then strode down that side toward the middle of the conference table.

And with his movement through the parting crowd, a hush spread through the hum of conversation.

One by one, curious faces turned his way.

The entire assembly took special note of his presence.

Interesting. He'd never quieted a packed room before.

Stopping before the gray upholstered armchair, he took another hearty gulp of coffee. Which had begun to cool toward warm.

All eyes remained glued on him.

A throat cleared. In the vicinity of the Joint Chiefs.

The gawkers began to shift attention away from him, toward the head of the table.

"This seat taken?" Rafe glanced down at the brunette.

"No idea." She turned to face the wall of monitors, giving a half shrug.

"Perfect." In every way.

Because he had a strong suspicion.

They—the two casual partygoers—had more in common than she realized.

Or maybe she realized more than she let on. And didn't like any of it.

What seemed crystal clear?

The chair had been saved for him, by them. His background hadn't been explained to her. And she chafed at everything going down that she didn't understand.

His presence had merely been the big, fat cherry on top of her clueless sundae.

"Do we know each other?" He rolled the chair back, swiveling the seat away from her, then eased down, nice and slow before rotating forward. No point in startling the natives.

"I've never seen you before." She took a tentative sip of coffee from a shiny black mug. Her pert nose wrinkled. A slender throat swallowed.

He swiveled his chair a little further around, in slight angle toward her. "You get the full-court press too?"

She sighed, ignoring his comment.

"Four stiff blue penguins." He tapped his left forefinger once on the brown sleeve of his coffee. "Helicopter ride. Jet flight. Quad-shot Americano pitstop."

That last got her attention. She stared toward his to-go cup. With longing.

"It's the best in town," he said, "according to the penguin squad."

"Anything's better than this piss," she muttered, shoving her mug toward the center of the table.

He nudged his cup between them. "Here. We can share."

She dropped him a *You've got to be kidding...* look.

"It's lukewarm. But got good flavor. And a kick." Kinda like her.

"*Okaaay...*" Wariness vibrated in her tone. "Thanks."

Accepting his olive branch as a truce, amid a scuffle that

he hadn't started, she worked the black plastic top off his cup, then took a sip.

Brunette hummed softly, swallowed, then gave him an arched-brows *It's good* nod.

He angled a *Told you...* nod back.

"Ladies and gentleman." The new Chairwoman of the Joint Chiefs of Staff, Lucille Miller, stood at the front of the room in her dark dress blues. "We've gathered you here today to address an unprecedented threat." She paused and stared down the line of seated individuals to her left. "Not just to the United States, but to Earth." Another lengthy pause as she swept a heavy gaze to those seated along Rafe's side. "To the survival of the human species."

"Sounds dire," he murmured.

After years of the entire world pulling humanity from the rubble from a hellacious coronavirus outbreak, what next?

Why all the NASA and Space Force types?

An alien invasion?

His brunette comrade glanced at him, arching her brows, as the chairwoman began to introduce those seated at the table, beginning on the opposite side. "Yes," she murmured.

He leaned closer. A faint scent wafted into his nose. Vanilla? Almond, maybe. Reminded him of a Christmas cookie. "Yes... what?"

"Yes, I got the 'full-court press.'"

"You a daredevil?" Brunette didn't strike him as the extreme-sport type.

Her brows furrowed, confusion making her pretty face a little adorable. "No." She snorted then leaned back in her chair. *C... I... A...* she mouthed.

"*Really.*" His brows arched. He didn't impress easily, but she didn't strike him as the spook type.

Glaring silence filled the room.

Both he and Brunette stared toward the chairwoman.

All eyes had landed on them.

"Mister Medina and Miss Finnerty, we apologize for all the mystery surrounding your invitation." A haughty glare lanced him, then speared *Miss* Finnerty. "But if the two of you would please pay attention, I'd like to only explain this once. We have a great amount of work to do. And not enough time to do it."

The chairwoman swept a more civil gaze round the table. "Mister Raphael Medina and Miss Calliope Finnerty have been recruited for their unique talents."

He cleared his throat. "Sorry for interrupting, but before we go any further, we need to clear up a few things. The name's Rafe. All I ever want to hear. Will not respond to anything else."

Madame Chairwoman dipped her head toward him in acknowledgment.

"Me too." His cohort straightened in her chair, squaring her shoulders. "It's Calli. And let's be honest here. I got ambushed at the library. And escorted halfway around the world."

Rafe thought about her dialect. "Washington state?"

Calli shook her head. "Rome."

Wow. Not remotely the answer he'd expected.

He glanced toward the chairwoman. "Neither of us were 'recruited.' More like drafted."

"We'd prefer your cooperation to be a choice," the chairwoman said, tone flat.

"And if we *don't* choose?" Defiance flared in his gut. That strong aversion to any kind of authority.

The chairwoman let out a heavy sigh. "Then, Mister Medina, the choice will be made...

For both of you."

Enjoy the rest of the adventure...
Quantanauts Genesis

ABOUT THE AUTHOR

Kat Bastion won several awards for her bestselling debut novel *Forged in Dreams and Magick.*

Kat & Stone Bastion's bestselling first novel *No Weddings* and the No Weddings series were named Best of 2014 by multiple romance review blogs.

When not defining love and redemption through scribed words, they enjoy hiking in vivid wildflower deserts, ancient tropical forests, and historic urban jungles.

Join our Bastion Family Adventurers!

Be in the know with preorder alerts, exclusive bonus gifts, and occasional free stories:

https://www.katbastion.com/email-subscription/

Let's be social...

CHARITY SUPPORT & AWARENESS

Your purchase of *Braving Soteria: A Quantanauts Collection* helps the victims of human trafficking because a portion of the net proceeds of all Kat & Stone Bastion's books are donated to charities who support them. These charities are creating legislation and prosecuting criminals, rescuing and restoring victims, and raising awareness in the effort to eradicate the tragedy of human trafficking.

"A single act of kindness is the foundation of many miracles."

— KAT BASTION, UTTERLY LOVED.